LEGION OF DORKS PRESENTS: LAUNDERED

An Anthology of Monster Messes

Edited by
KELLY LYNN COLBY

Cursed Dragon Ship
PUBLISHING

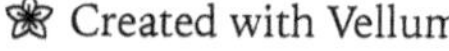 Created with Vellum

To those who clean up other people's messes. The world would be a wreck without you.

INTRODUCTION

Kevin and I met the 2Dorks, Stephen and Ashley, at Dragon Con in Atlanta in 2017. It was a random encounter outside Ted's restaurant while we were waiting to be seated. On the way home, we listened to their podcast, *Horseshoes and Hand Grenades*, in which they cover silly and ridiculous news from across the world. By the time we reached Houston, we were fans.

As it turns out, these amazing people—including Jacob, their producer—are the heart and soul of the Legion of Dorks (LoD). They've connected a group of creative gamers on a Discord channel to talk about life, the universe, and everything. The channel's not just for gamers. Technical knowledge is shared, along with opinions on music and movies.

The cool thing is the Legion of Dorks isn't only a place to hang out. We've become friends. Through our interactions, I discovered that many voices in the group have incredible stories to tell and full imaginations to bring them to life. I thought it would be a fascinating experiment to set those minds loose with only a theme—and a word count—to keep them restrained and see what they create. Jacob came up with an awesome title and we ran with it.

The result is what you're holding in your hand now. *Laundered: An*

Anthology of Monster Messes was conceived and filled by the minds of the Legion of Dorks community with help from a few outsiders. All profit, after costs of production, will go straight to the LoD Gaming and Giving Charity Drive.

We at Cursed Dragon Ship Publishing, LLC, have been honored to team with the 2Dorks to make this book a reality. We hope you enjoy the adventures within.

Kelly Lynn Colby

Editorial Director Cursed Dragon Ship Publishing, LLC

A WELCOMED MESS

Stephanie Adams

*S*tan stared incredulously into the giant pair of round, dilated eyeballs looking up at him. It was three in the morning, and his brother had showed up on his doorstep unannounced, with a cage containing a small pink fur ball with eyes.

"Now explain to me again why I have to take care of this thing for you?"

"Come on, man. I just got the call this evening. This is a once-in-a-lifetime opportunity. Being featured in the *Journal of Exotic Beasts* is like the culmination of my photography career. I would have Audrey watch Princess, but she's out of town until next week."

Stan sighed and took hold of the metal handle of Princess's cage.

"Oh, man! Thank you! Thank you! You have no idea what this means to me." Stan's brother, Dylan, bounced up and down like a schoolgirl who had just won tickets to a Justin Bieber concert. "Okay, so she needs fresh water every day. And don't worry about letting her out of her cage. She's a beast to have to catch and somewhat of an escape artist." Dylan thoughtfully furrowed his brow for a moment and paused. "Anyway, just feed her whatever scraps from the table you have leftover. She's not picky."

Stan couldn't help but wonder what his wife would think of the fluorescent hair ball eating her prized beef bourguignon.

"And *no one* can know you have Princess, Stan. Seriously. It's the most important thing. Not even Charlotte. Princess isn't exactly what you would call legal in the US right now."

"Great," Stan said sarcastically. He felt a twinge of anxiety. He was running for mayor, and the last thing he needed was to be handling anything illegal, much less a devious tiny monster. "Anything else?"

"Here's information on how to get in touch with me and where I'll be staying." Dylan handed Stan a thin stack of papers. "I put Princess's favorite blanket in the cage with her. Sometimes she gets homesick, and she likes the smell of it. I should be back in town by Thursday to get her. And thanks again. You have no idea what this means to me." Dylan awkwardly embraced both Stan and Princess in a big bear hug.

Stan sleepily nodded to Dylan as he shut the door. "Okay. Be safe. Get good pictures.

"And don't get eaten," he muttered under his breath. He looked down at Princess "Well, girl. Looks like it's just you and me for the next three days."

Princess cooed.

Stan figured the safest place to hide Princess would be in his gentleman's cave. He refused to call it a man cave. That name brought to mind images of sports memorabilia strewn across dirty walls, old Berber carpet, and a distinct smell of nacho cheese and beer. Stan's gentleman's cave featured a 92" flat screen TV, shining hardwood floors, plush leather couches, and a pool table—everything one would imagine in the basement of a lawyer and a pillar of the community.

Stan loved his town, where all the lawns were mowed to the appropriate height, everyone knew everyone else's name, and the ladies met not only monthly for gardening club but also weekly for recipe sharing. In fact, he loved it so much, he was running for mayor. He would easily win too if it weren't for Robert S. Schumaker, or Bert as he was known. Like being called Bert instead of Robert made him more approachable or something.

Stan couldn't stand Bert. Bert was a hypocrite who was in everyone else's business. Stan wanted nothing more than to beat him for mayor.

But for now, what Stan wanted more than anything was sleep. He had spent that entire Sunday campaigning and was beginning to feel the 3:00 a.m. wakeup call from his brother.

He sat Princess down in a corner of the room where she would have good airflow and plenty to look at. Stan's wife, Charlotte—or Lotti, as he lovingly called her—never came down to his gentleman's cave, so he didn't need to worry about hiding her. He patted the top of her cage, wished her good night, and retired to his room.

He glanced at his clock before dozing off: 4:30 a.m.

Perfect.

*S*tan's alarm clock sang the song of its people at 6:00 a.m.

Shut up, shut up, shut up.

He reached over to throw his alarm clock across the room and roll over, but then he remembered he had an appointment with Harold Drake in a couple of hours. Harold was a banker and one of Stan's most important clients. He begrudgingly dragged himself out of bed, careful not to wake his wife, who was still snoring. He grabbed his navy silk robe and slippers and stumbled down the stairs toward the kitchen. He was going through the day's agenda in his head when something cold and hard popped under his foot, jolting him back to reality.

What the hell?

He didn't want to look down. *A Ping-Pong ball? No, Ping-Pong balls don't pop like that. A giant spider? Dear God. What if it was one of those wolf spiders that carry their babies on their back? The baby spiders would have dispersed like a million miniature nightmares all over the kitchen.*

Stan practically levitated off the floor and fell backward over their $5,000 Restoration Hardware leather couch, his feet dangling above his head. A small gelatinous blob slithered down the sole of his foot and splattered directly onto his forehead.

Egg?

He looked at his foot.

Egg! It was just an egg.

Wait. An egg? Why was there an egg in the middle of the kitchen?

Stan clumsily rolled off the couch and peeked into the kitchen. It was an absolute disaster. It looked like a hungry grizzly bear that hadn't eaten in four days had discovered a Twinkie factory.

Princess.

It had to be Princess. That was the only explanation Stan could think of. That, and he vaguely remembered Dylan complaining of this exact situation when he had first brought Princess home from Thailand.

Stan jumped up and started cleaning as fast as he could. Lotti couldn't see this mess. That would mean questions. And questions would inevitably lead to Stan having to tell Lotti about Princess.

"*What* in the seven circles of hell happened here, Stanley Richfield?"

Crap.

"Bacon."

"Excuse me?"

Stan couldn't bring himself to look at Lotti, but he knew from the tone of her voice she most assuredly had a hand on her hip. "Bacon. I was looking for the bacon."

"Oh, I see." Lotti paused. "So you felt it necessary to empty our entire refrigerator and trash the kitchen to find bacon? Something we haven't even had in the house for the last six months due to your elevated triglycerides?"

"Cholesterol."

"What?"

"Elevated cholesterol. Cholesterol is different from triglycer—"

"Whatever, Stanley! I have a booster club luncheon this afternoon to discuss our yearly fundraiser, and I promised them chocolate souf-flé. You know what I can't make without eggs? *Chocolate soufflé!*"

Maybe it was that her hair was twisted up in curlers like little devil serpents, maybe it was the bits of mud mask from the night before she still had on her face, or maybe it was the tears welling up in her eyes, but Stan felt some weird combination of fear of and pity for Lotti. He also didn't want her asking any more questions about the dirty kitchen. He'd do anything to keep her from prying and finding out about Princess.

"Why don't I go to the grocery store and grab a few more eggs. If I go right now, I should still be able to make that appointment with Mr. Drake this morning."

She immediately perked up. "Really? Oh, will you also pick up a few bars of that lovely new dark chocolate the store just got in? I was thinking of trying something new with the soufflé this time."

"Of course, dear."

Lotti trotted up the stairs to get ready for the day. As soon as Stan was sure she couldn't see or hear him, he dashed to his gentleman's cave to search for Princess. He was expecting a huge mess in there as well, but all was tidy and calm. Princess was peacefully sleeping in her cage. She cooed a little every time she breathed out. Stan investigated the cage. Nothing was out of place.

Huh. Wonder how she got out. Dylan hadn't been kidding about her being an escape artist. *But why didn't she* stay *out?* Stan thoughtfully scrunched up his face.

It must be the blanket Dylan left with her in the cage. She had returned to the familiar smell and comfort of the blanket. She missed Dylan. She might have been a terror, but she was a sentimental terror. Stan placed an extra lock on the door of Princess's cage for added security before heading to the store. He couldn't be too careful. After all, she was illegal.

Stan sped the five miles to the grocery store. He still had an hour and a half before his appointment with Mr. Drake. He was stalking the aisles, trying to remember where the dark chocolate was, when he heard an all-too-familiar voice.

"Stanley?"

Stan had been so focused on the mess at home and on Princess that he had completely forgotten he was still in his robe and slippers and was covered in a breakfast buffet's worth of food. Something he was now acutely aware of.

He slowly spun around, sporting an exaggerated, somewhat garish smile. "Francine! Fancy seeing you here so early! Oh, and you too, Bert. What a coincidence!"

Well, yippee skippy.

The two worst possible people to bump into in his current condition just happened to be shopping at the same market as him at 6:30 a.m. Who shops for groceries at six thirty in the morning? Stan was okay with Bert being there because, well, frankly he didn't give a crap what Bert thought. But Francine? She was the matriarch of the entire community. Francine had lived in Willow Springs since before they had phone lines. She was regent of the local chapter of Daughters of the American Revolution (DAR), had served on the town council, organized practically all the festivals and fairs, and was pretty much the deciding factor on who would be elected as the next mayor.

"Well, yes." She forced a meager smile. "We have a DAR meeting this afternoon, and I was doing some last-minute shopping for my scones. I was in the baking aisle when I bumped into Bert here." She hesitated a moment, then cocked her head slightly, like an inquisitive King Charles Spaniel. "Is everything okay, Stan?"

"Yeah," chimed in Bert. "You look like a cooking show gone bad, Stan my man."

"What? Yeah! Everything's great. I just dropped a few eggs this morning making breakfast, so Lotti didn't have enough to make her chocolate soufflé. Being the amazing husband I am," he winked at Francine, "I told her I would run out and grab them." He chuckled uneasily.

"Well, then, how kind of you. Tell Lotti I said I'll see her

Wednesday at book club." Francine flapped her saggy, bejeweled hand in Stan's direction. "Till next time."

"Always a pleasure seeing you, Francine. Tell your wonderful husband I said hello. I hope he has a nice trip this week." He smiled politely at the antique of a woman standing in front of him. Then he directed his gaze at his nemesis. "Bert."

"Stan."

Stan made a beeline for the cash register, then hurried home. Lotti met him at the door.

"Did you find my dark chocolate?"

"No, but I did find Francine Harrington and Bert Schumaker." He huffed.

Lotti looked annoyed that Stan hadn't brought her what she had requested, but the annoyance quickly changed to intrigue. "What the heck were they doing there at six thirty in the morning?"

Definitely not shopping for eggs that an illegal pink fluff ball devoured the night before, Stan mused.

"No idea. I think Francine said something about scones for DAR." Stan did his best impression of Francine and flapped his hand at Lotti. "She also said she's looking forward to seeing you at book club this Wednesday."

"Oh my gosh, Stanley! I just remembered, I forgot to tell Francine that the book club meeting was changed from Wednesday to Saturday. Carrie Beth had a funeral or something to go to, and we had to move it. She was going to make those lovely scones to bring to the book club. If you see her in town again today, would you please let her know, dear? I'm so busy this afternoon, I don't have time, and the old codger doesn't have a cell phone or email."

Lotti giggled to herself. Stan figured calling Francine an old codger had made her feel like one of those bad girls in her favorite soap opera. Granted, she would never say anything like that to Francine's face. He also figured she felt bad for saying it the moment the words left her mouth. Poor Lotti didn't have a bad bone in her body. Bless her.

"Of course I will, honey."

Stan gave Lotti a quick peck on her cheek, making her squeal as if a rat had just laid a very large turd on her favorite pair of Kate Spade heels. He chuckled at her reaction. He was still that little boy who had chased his school crush with slimy frogs.

"Gross, Stanley. You still have egg and Lord knows what else all over you!" Lotti flicked her hand in Stan's direction. "Go get your shower."

Stan couldn't help but notice a slight grin on Lotti's face. Even after thirteen years, he still loved making her grin like that. Stan rushed upstairs to grab a quick shower and hurry to his morning appointment.

The office was abuzz with people typing, printers working, and phones ringing. Stan was using the office not only for his law practice but also as his campaign headquarters. His partner had not been ecstatic about this. However, he had finally agreed to it after Stan told him he could be the town crier at the Christmas Festival if Stan won. While it was a much-sought-after position, Stan couldn't fathom why anyone would want the job. The outfit alone made him cringe—a 1700s ensemble, complete with high-heeled shoes and puffy sleeves that would make any avant-garde designer cringe.

Stan cheerfully greeted his employees as he made his way to his office. Mr. Drake was waiting for him.

Stan smiled politely. "I hope you didn't have to wait long."

Mr. Drake returned the smile and shook his head. "Only just got here. I was held up by that gossip Darcy Chillton. Say, did you hear about what happened down on Thurston Street?"

"No, what?" Stan cocked his head as he removed his folders and notes from his briefcase.

"Apparently, a burglar hit up two cafés and the bakery. They didn't steal anything, just made a mess of the place and ate half the inventory. People said they were surprised whoever did it could fit through the doors after their escapade." Harold chuckled as he shifted in his chair.

"No way! Why would anyone do that?" Stan tried his best to act bewildered as panic set in. Could it have been Princess? Man, was he screwed if it was Princess. "Do they have any idea who it was?" He tried to act as nonchalant as possible.

"No, but they said the pilferer had to have been an expert lockpick. There was no sign of forced entry. They did find something weird at each place, though."

This is it, thought Stan. *It's over.* He stared at Mr. Drake, pretending to look puzzled. "Yeah? What's that?"

"Pink fur."

Stan froze. "Pink fur?"

"I dunno. Maybe the thief has an affinity for pink fur coats." Mr. Drake let out a big hearty laugh. "Anyway, you can't really trust anything Darcy Chillton says. She'd devise any story to make you think she knows about everything going on in this town.

"So, how are the legal documents you're drawing up looking?"

Wait. Was that it? No more questions? It was just being brushed off? Stan couldn't believe how lucky he was. He finished up his meeting with Mr. Drake, then made a call to the police department to determine what they knew about the burglaries. Stan was transferred to a detective working the case, who informed him the case was on the back burner. There was little evidence and more important cases to investigate. Stan let out a sigh of relief.

Everything is going to be okay.

***

Stan loved Tuesdays. He got to sleep in on Tuesdays. He got the whole house to himself on Tuesdays. He could do whatever he wanted on Tuesdays. Upon merging their businesses, Stan and his law partner had decided they would each get one weekday off. Tuesdays were his.

Stan stretched, rolled out of bed, and leisurely threw on some comfortable clothes. He made his way to the kitchen for a hot cup of coffee and the newspaper. He was enjoying the business section when the doorbell rang.

"Darn solicitors," he grumbled. "One day, I'm going to give them an earful."

Stan cracked the door just enough for half his face to poke through. "What is it?" he asked smugly.

"Hey, Mr. Richfield. It's Hunter. I hate to bother you, but you're the only one I knew would be home. I was working on the neighbor's yard and noticed that—"

"We already have a gardener, Hunter. Thank you." Stan started closing the door before he was even finished with his sentence.

The teenage son of a neighbor who lived a few houses down, Hunter had started a landscaping and yard care service over the summer and was actually doing quite well for himself. Stan wished he had thought of the idea when he was a teenager. Maybe he wouldn't still be paying off his law school loans.

"No, wait! That's not what I'm here for, sir. I need you to come see this. There aren't any flowers left. It's like a deer came through and ate them all. Except they're *all* gone, so it would have had to have been either a really large deer or, like, fifty of them." Hunter looked extremely confused.

"What?" Stan opened the door and popped his head outside to look at his roses.

Nothing. Zilch. Nada. Every single beautiful creamy white bloom was gone. All that was left were stems and thorns. Stan loved his roses. He tended to them regularly, had someone come out and water them while the family was on vacation, and took pride in displaying them at the summer flower festival.

"My roses!" he cried out, practically tackling Hunter to the ground so he could investigate.

"It's not just your roses, Mr. Richfield. Look." Hunter pointed down the street.

Every single bright blossom, bud, and flower was gone. Everything was just green—boring, plain green. What could have done this? *Who* would have done this? It made no sense. Then, suddenly, it did. Stan spotted a small pink blob of fur in the ocean of green.

Princess.

Stan was learning an awful lot about his brother's fluffy, gluttonous outlaw. The newest realization was that Princess truly did eat *anything* and that she was obviously nocturnal. Now he had to think of a story to cover up her latest gastric antics.

"Well, Hunter. I hate to say it, but I've seen this before." Stan attempted to look like he knew what he was talking about.

"What? Really?" Hunter looked skeptical.

"Yep. It's been a while, but I've definitely experienced this before. Every thirty years, a swarm of beetles descends upon our town. They're called..." He paused for a minute, looking for a truly convincing name. "Budder beetles."

Crap! No! That's not convincing. That's absolutely idiotic. It sounds like "butter beetles." You would think a lawyer would be able to come up with something a little less ridiculous. Quick. Fix it.

"Now, I know what you're thinking: 'That's a stupid name.' But it's not, if you think about it. Budder beetles eat flowers and buds, therefore the name. They truly are a menace. So much so that no one ever really likes to talk about them." Stan hoped Hunter was better at gardening than he was at rationalizing. "They come out of the ground at night, eat all the flowers, and then disappear again for another thirty years. They're only local to this area. It's the weirdest thing."

Hunter just stood there, confused and not knowing how to respond. "Okay, Mr. Richfield. That sounds... interesting. I'll have to look into it. Have a good day."

Stan could tell Hunter was just giving up rather than attempting to make sense of what he had just been told. It didn't matter, though. He had made it another day without having to explain the mess. He slammed the door shut and bolted for his gentleman's cave to check on the fur ball. Once again, Princess was a tranquil blob of fluff, sleeping and cooing away. Stan sighed and investigated her cage once more. He had to make sure there was no way she could escape again—

a feat that would be easier if he knew how the heck she was getting out in the first place.

He remembered then that Dylan had left him with information regarding his flights, his hotels, and numbers to get in touch with him in an emergency. He found the papers and began rummaging through them. Bingo! He was able to find the number for the cell phone Dylan's publisher had given him to take on the trip.

Stan grabbed his cell phone and dialed.

"Hello?" It was Dylan.

"Hey, Dylan, it's Stan."

"Stan! Oh my gosh, dude. It's so amazing here. This has been the most incredible experience of my life. Do you know what I just got done photographing?"

"That's nice, Dylan. But I'm having a slight problem with Princess."

"She's getting out, isn't she?"

"Yep."

"Damn. I was afraid of that."

"So how do I keep her in?"

Silence.

"Dylan?"

"Yeah?"

"How do I keep her in? She's already wreaked havoc on the neighborhood, and she's only been here two days."

Silence.

"Dylan!" Stan was getting impatient.

"So, the Thai people had some special herb they put around her cage that kept her in. She didn't like the smell or something. I didn't think it was a big deal, so I never asked what it was. So now she just kind of does her own thing."

"What do you mean, 'she just kind of does her own thing'?" Stan was beginning to get irritated with his free-spirited, fly-by-the-seat-of-his-pants brother.

"I mean, she just comes and goes as she pleases. I have noticed that if you feed her a big healthy meal before bed, she doesn't roam as far." He paused. "I'm sorry, man. I knew if I told you she got out regularly, you wouldn't take her."

"Of course I wouldn't take her. You do know I'm in the middle of a campaign right now, right? I can't risk this sort of scandal." Stan's blood was boiling.

"Okay, okay. Just calm down. You sound like a crazy politician or something. It's just a mayoral race. I'll come back early to get her. I've actually been ahead of schedule most of the trip, so I can be there tomorrow afternoon."

"Fine."

"Fine!"

Stan heard the whimsical chimes of his doorbell coming from upstairs. "I've got to go. Someone's at the door. I'll see you tomorrow afternoon." He was so angry, he hung up the phone without giving Dylan the chance to say goodbye.

So much for his relaxing Tuesday. He tromped upstairs, annoyed but thankful that things would be going to be back to normal the next day. Once again, he cracked the door and stuck his nose out.

"Yes?" he grumbled.

"Stan?" A soft but stern voice questioned.

"Francine!"

Why? She was like the grim reaper, except she only appeared at really unfortunate, embarrassing times. Although by this point, Stan wished she really was the grim reaper; he'd rather be dead than be where he was right then. He opened the door and stepped outside.

"Your house was to be featured in the Willow Springs parade of homes. I've already discussed all the details with Lotti. I was just stopping by to see if I could help with the preparations. However, it looks like you have had a… complication with your landscaping."

"Yeah. Well, you know, budder beetles." Stan chuckled.

"What?" Francine scrunched her face up so hard, Stan was sure all the injected silicone would squirt out at him.

"Oh, it's nothing. Hunter knows what I'm talking about."

Francine stared at him blankly.

"I think it was deer, Francine. Like, a whole herd of them or something. It's truly unfortunate, and I honestly don't know what to do. I mean, look." He pointed down the street. "No one on this street has any flowers left."

Stan spotted a plump, sweaty man in a tracksuit power walking up the sidewalk.

Of course, it was Bert.

"Stan my man! What's with the shrubbery?" Sweat poured down Bert's face and sprayed into the air every time he opened his mouth to talk.

Stan thought he was going to be sick.

"Apparently, a herd of deer ate all the street's flora." Francine turned to look at Stan as though waiting for a better explanation.

Bert had obviously not noticed Francine until she spoke.

"Francine!" Bert sashayed up the walk to the house. "So good to see you!" He leaned in uncomfortably close to Francine. "You know, there may not be any flowers on the shrubs, but who needs them when I have the prettiest blossom of all right beside me." He winked at Francine. Stan wasn't sure if it was a legitimate wink or he just had sweat dripping into his eye.

Francine giggled and waved her hand dismissively. "You're so kind, Bert. Say, I've heard nothing but good things about the new fountain you've had installed in your front yard. Would you mind if I came by and had a look? We'll be needing an alternate home to showcase in the parade of homes due to the insatiable wildlife that apparently stalks this street."

"I would be honored!" crowed Bert. He glanced sideways at Stan as if to say, "Suck it, pal."

"Wonderful!" exclaimed Francine. "Tell Lotti I said hello, Stan. Till next time."

"Always a pleasure seeing you, Francine." He hesitated. "Bert."

"Stan."

Stan didn't want Lotti to come home that evening. He didn't want to have to tell her they would no longer be showcased in the parade of homes. He knew it would break her heart, and because she had no idea he was the cause of it, he felt even more guilty. He was sitting in the kitchen, contemplating how he was going to explain it to her, when she walked in the door.

"Hi, sweetheart!" She beamed. "How was your day off?"

"Not as good as it should have been," Stan lamented. He decided to just come right out with it. "We're not going to be showcased in the parade of homes, honey."

"Oh." She stared at the floor and dropped her purse onto the counter.

"I'm so sorry, sweetie. I'm not sure what happened, but all the flowers on the street have been eaten up by . . . something . . . and Francine decided to choose another house to showcase. I know you were so excited about it. I wish there was something I could do." He walked over to her and rubbed her delicate hand.

"Screw it!" she said, perking up. "I wasn't looking forward to polishing all our silver to display anyway. And who does Francine think she is? It's called parade of homes, not parade of lawns."

Stan suddenly remembered why he had fallen in love with Lotti. She was incredibly resilient. "So you're not upset?"

"Not at all." She grinned at Stan lovingly. "Actually, why don't we celebrate by ordering in tonight and watching a movie?"

"That would be wonderful." He hugged Lotti.

"Let's watch *Steel Magnolias* again. I just love that movie."

Stan cringed on the inside. *Dear Lord, not again.* "Whatever makes you happy."

"Oh!" Lotti gasped. "Did you let Francine know we moved the book club when you saw her?"

"No, dear. I honestly didn't think of it at the time. I'll let her know the next time I see her. I promise."

Everything was going to be okay. He only had to keep Princess through tomorrow afternoon, then things would be back to normal. Nothing too catastrophic had happened. He was sure he could make up for the unfortunate events that had occurred over the last few days. In fact, his Tuesday had shaped up to be a decent day.

Well, maybe except for the choice of movie.

*S*tan was suddenly jarred awake by a loud, metallic crash outside. He and Lotti had fallen asleep on the couch watching *Steel Magnolias*—for the third time that month. He looked over at Lotti to see if the sound had woken her as well. She hadn't moved an inch and was, in fact, drooling all over the couch.

Sound asleep. Like a little, rabid cherubim.

Stan sat up and listened carefully to be sure he wasn't just dreaming.

Clang. Clink. THUNK.

Yep. Not a dream. He jumped up and grabbed the closest thing he could find that would suffice as a weapon, which just happened to be an old golf umbrella he had found while cleaning out the coat closet earlier that day. Slipping on his shoes, he slunk down the hallway to the back porch, where the sound was coming from.

Something was in his trash. A raccoon, maybe? Hoping to catch the culprit, he turned on the porch light and flung open the back door in one swift motion. Trash was strewn across his back porch. There was no sign of the offender.

Then it hit him. He had fallen asleep on the couch with Lotti after dinner and had completely forgotten to feed Princess. He usually fed her table scraps after Lotti went to sleep. She was going to be ravenous. This was surely the end of him and his campaign for mayor. He could only imagine what Princess was doing right now.

He heard another clink down the street. Another trash can. Maybe he could catch her.

Stan raced down the street and into the next, then the next, then the next. He was trying desperately to keep up with Princess. Finally, he closed in on her on the back patio of an enormous, palatial house. He had run around in so many circles, and it was so dark, he had no idea where he was or whose house he was behind.

Clink. Thunk! Down went the trash can.

And down with you, Princess! thought Stan as he lunged for the trash can. A pastel pouf zipped past Stan, through the backyard, and back down the street.

Seriously?

He was done chasing her. He was going to just let her run amok, ruin the town, and then move the next day. As nosy as the neighborhood was, he was sure they would trace everything back to him.

He stood up, brushed half-eaten stuffed grape leaves off his shirt and started for home. Wherever that was.

Suddenly, the house's floodlights illuminated. He turned toward the door and froze like a deer in headlights. More like a herd of deer that had allegedly eaten a home improvement store's worth of roses. The back door creaked open. Stan stared at the doorway, unable to move. Why wouldn't his legs work?

"Stanley?"

Francine. It was Francine. He blinked a couple of times to be sure. Oh, yeah. It was definitely Francine. She was standing in the doorway, squinting against the harsh white light, dressed in nothing but a pink robe.

"Stanley, is that you?" she asked again. "What in heaven's name are you doing here at this time of night?"

"Good evening, Francine," he said politely. He thought of every reasonable excuse he could come up with for being behind her house in the middle of the night, then settled on the most useful one. "Lotti wanted me to let you know that, due to a funeral, Carrie Beth cannot attend book club tomorrow and it has been moved to next Saturday. I forgot to tell you when I saw you earlier today. Have a wonderful night."

He began to walk away when he remembered that Lotti had wanted to make sure Francine also knew to bring her scones. He sighed and wheeled around to remind her to bring her famous confections.

That's when it happened.

Bert, in all his hairy, rotund glory, stepped around the corner and into the frame of view, wearing nothing but a black silk G-string.

"It was that blasted raccoon I've been telling you about, wasn't it, darlin'?" Bert strutted up to Francine, wrapped his shaggy arm around her, and then peered out the door.

His eyes met Stan's. No one said a word. They all stood motionless, staring at each other.

Stan decided to break the silence. "Francine, Lotti also wanted me to remind you to bring your much-anticipated scones to the event." He paused for a moment, taking in the deplorable sight in front of him. "Always a pleasure seeing you, Francine."

Francine frowned.

"Bert," he sneered.

"Stan."

The next morning, Stan was once again startled out of his sleep. Lotti was squealing and bouncing up and down, holding a tray of breakfast foods. Orange juice sloshed everywhere, but she didn't seem to care.

"Good morning, Mr. Mayor!"

"Huh?" Stan rubbed his eyes.

"A little birdy from DAR called and told me that Bert Schumaker has dropped out of the race, *and* that Francine Harrington has pledged to endorse you for mayor! You're the only one running now, honey. You're going to be mayor!"

Stan couldn't believe it. Apparently, being caught having an affair with the one person who could single-handedly decide who won the race was more of a scandal than an illegal monster from Thailand stealing and vandalizing the neighborhood. For the first time, Stan was actually thankful he had helped his brother out.

That afternoon, Dylan came to pick Princess up as promised.

"You know what, Dylan? She's really not that bad." Stan handed Dylan the cage.

"Yeah, she's pretty cute, huh? I want you to know how much I appreciate you doing this for me, man. I really am sorry about the mess, though."

"You know, Dylan, over the last few days, I've learned that, sometimes, it doesn't matter how hard you try to be orderly and organized; messes still happen. You just have to learn to welcome them into your life. In fact," he smiled, "they may just end up making everything else fall right into place."

TOAST

Jacob Hartsell

"Dammit to Hades and back, Max. Why is Bob dead?"

Death looked down at Max, who was currently cowering in obvious fear. The teen had tucked himself into a corner of the room and refused to meet her eyes.

"I'm sorry," Max squeaked. "It really was an accident."

"How does a monster accidentally murder a human?" Death asked, her restraint slipping. "Bob was not on the *list*."

Flicking her gaze to the tablet she held in her hands, she noted that, according to the Master Plan, Bob still had thirty-six years, eighty-seven days, fourteen hours, six minutes, and nine seconds to go.

Death bit the inside of her cheek. If the Boss found out a non-listed individual had been harvested, there was no telling what he would do. Literally. No one could ever tell what the Boss was capable of. It completely depended on his mood that day. He was a mercurial S.O.B.

She needed to clean this mess up before someone had to clean her up.

Death had successfully managed unsanctioned killings in the past, but it was a chaotic, convoluted, and craptastic method she was surprised even worked. A tapestry of deception was woven to mask each transgression, which became progressively harder every time a glitch was introduced.

"Max," Death hissed, side-eyeing the young monster, "walk me through how it was an *accident* that you tore Bob's arms off and beat him to death with them."

Max's already too-large eyes bulged wider. "It's all a blur," he said, his fluffy hide trembling.

Pressing her flaming-red lips together, Death fought the urge to send Max into the void for a decade or two as punishment. Young monsters needed patience and guidance. Max was lacking the latter because his father worked tirelessly for her as an Envoy. So technically, this was Death's fault.

A cleanup of this type would involve a patch, which wasn't normally that big a deal, assuming it was authorized. Bob's patch would *not* be authorized and therefore an abject pain in the arse. Before Death could even actively worry about the patching step, though, Bob's mangled body had to be cleaned and repaired.

Great.

She never knew ahead of time if the fix required for a mess like this would integrate seamlessly enough to go undetected, as every glitch produced a ripple effect. Most were innocuous, leaving the Master Plan relatively unchanged, but some had the capacity to stuff up the timeline completely.

Death would need help for this particular glitch. Bob had been mangled to the point of needing an expert, and his spirit was already in the aether.

As she contemplated, she balked, realizing she'd have to call Viktor. The man was difficult to read and tended to be an absolute hard-ass, but he did good work. If the barrier separating monsters and humans was breached, Viktor was there to smooth things over.

Huffing an annoyed sigh, Death made the call, trying not to grit her teeth while the ringtone beeped back at her.

"Death," Viktor said by way of greeting.

"I need your services," she replied curtly. "We have a glitch."

When Viktor spoke again, his tone had changed, and she could hear the *tsk* of his tongue against the roof of his mouth. Smug bastard.

Death popped the bones in her neck before giving him the address.

"I'll be there in ten minutes," Viktor replied.

Nine minutes and thirty-seven seconds later, a knock on the door echoed through the house.

"You look radiant, as always," Viktor said, peering over Death's shoulder into the entryway.

Death *was* radiant, but not in a mundane, "you must have been on vacation recently" way. Her job came with certain perks. She was attractive to everyone, human and monster. It was hard to do her job when people were constantly running away, so tweaks had been made over the centuries.

She had the ability to shift her appearance depending on what the situation required. It was a clever piece of magic the Boss had entrusted to her years ago.

Currently, her slick brunette hair was strewn with locks of gold that echoed her milk-and-coffee skin. Dark lashes fluttered over large brown eyes flecked with green, and large lips pouted slightly down at the corners. Her uniform of white on white had her in only barely comfortable leather pants, a V-neck top that dipped a little too low, and a white leather overcoat that dusted the tops of her knees. White gloves and cherry-red stilettos that matched her lipstick completed the ridiculous getup that years of research claimed made her more approachable.

"I appreciate the haste," Death said with a small smile.

"If you're calling me, I assume it's important," Viktor said, stepping past Death.

She shrugged, the leather of her overcoat creaking slightly. "It's not the end of the world. It's just irritating. A juvenile monster committed an unsanctioned killing."

Viktor adjusted the lapels of his charcoal-gray jacket and looked down his nose at Death. "That is your responsibility, not mine."

Death bit her tongue on a sharp reply. Viktor was right; she was responsible for every human and monster death. She didn't cause deaths, so much as coordinate them until they fit into the Master Plan. No one entity could possibly keep up with the number of deaths that occurred every single day, so she relied on hired monsters called Envoys to help execute her orders.

"It will ultimately be both our problems if this goes unchecked."

Curving his lips in a wolfish smile, Viktor nodded. "So you say. Who else is here?"

"Bob's daughter. Dreamers are keeping her down until we're done here."

Death lead Viktor to the second floor and down the hallway to the bedroom, where Max decided to go accidentally homicidal. The acrid, musty air tickled Viktor's nose, causing him to wrinkle it in protest.

The petite man sighed and adjusted his lapels. Streaks of blood were strewn across the walls in a Jackson Pollock–like manner. Humans were fragile things, but this one would take a week to put back properly.

"That... is an impressive amount of blood."

Death cast a scathing look at poor Max, who still cowered in the corner.

"I am so sorry. It was an accident," Max repeated.

Viktor raised an eyebrow and looked at Death. "Hell of an accident," he said softly.

"I didn't want to kill him," Max said, almost pleading. "He saw me, and I panicked. I didn't know what to do. He was scared and started screaming. I just wanted him to calm down. He was so loud."

Viktor scrunched his nose again and motioned for the duo to follow him from the room. No reason to be uncomfortable. He gave the fluffy blue teen a once-over. "Why were you even here?"

Max shifted his magenta eyes toward Death before casting them down to the floor. "I'd rather not say," he whispered sheepishly.

"I'd rather not be here cleaning up your mess, Max," responded Death. "So I think you will say whether you want to or not."

Max shifted in discomfort and flexed his claws in and out. "I wanted to see Rose."

Viktor narrowed his eyes. "Rose?"

"Bob's daughter," Max mumbled, nodding his head toward the bedroom the Dreamers were in.

Highly paid and highly full of themselves, Dreamers replaced unwanted thoughts with those deemed safe. They pulled sightings of monsters from human minds and replaced them with animals of similar size.

Death let her lips part in annoyed shock. It was forbidden for monsters to consort with humans. There were exceptions, but romance was not one of them.

Viktor shook his head in distaste. "Location of the spirit?"

"We don't have it yet."

"Of course. How many years did he have left?

"Thirty-six," she muttered angrily.

A muscle in Viktor's jaw tightened. "The Master Plan—"

"Is totally stuffed, I know," Death stated.

"We're patching a sliver, then?" asked Viktor

"That's the only way I see out of this," she replied, pouting slightly.

"I assume you will collect it?"

Death nodded. Collecting a spirit sliver wasn't an easy task, though, as it had to be done relatively quickly.

Each minute Bob was out of his body was a lost memory for his spirit. If Bob's spirit lost enough memories, he would come back a completely different person. The longer a spirit was in the aether, the smaller it became and the more memories it would shed; eventually, it would become small enough to be considered a sliver. Putting a sliver back into a body was bad news as someone *always* noticed the change.

Friends who suddenly stopped drinking, family members who decided to take up skydiving after always being afraid of heights, sisters who went from tomboy to playboy overnight: they were all slivers who'd been put back into their old bodies.

"Who do you have programming?" asked Viktor

"Roman," Death said shortly.

That was assuming Death could even locate the spirit.

Roman's job would be to hack the spirit and locate Bob's memories. Once he gained access to the memories, Roman could review them for completeness and edit them to patch any gaps. Missing memories were typically replaced with overgeneralized, nondescript memories. As long as they were vague enough, no one ever really noticed, but the bigger the patch, the bigger the issue. If the patch was too large, Roman would have to get creative and implant memories that matched the spirit's personality as closely as possible.

Roman was a great programmer, but even he had his limits. If Roman rushed—which he was going to have to—those patched thoughts and memories could change Bob's personality.

Death stared down at the short man by her side. Finally, she whispered, "I don't want to be retired because of this."

In a rare show of fidelity, Viktor placed a hand on Death's shoulder, which made her even more uneasy.

"Call Roman," Viktor said. "After I collect what's left of Bob here, I'll get the body prepped for programming."

"Is the body repairable?" Death asked, hoping that Bob wasn't too far gone for even their best.

Viktor's thin lips twitched up at one side. "I'm not sure there's enough skill in the world to fix it."

Max squeaked another apology.

Death frowned, her brows pulling down over her heavy lashes. "We can implant memories for smaller scars," she said, thinking out loud.

"He's missing his arms," Viktor said frankly. "That's gonna be one hell of a memory patch."

"I have faith in you," Death said with a lightness she didn't feel. If they failed to patch Bob back into existence, the Boss would surely notice. The thought made her shudder.

"Here's to hope," Death said with a mock toast to Viktor. *Hope had better come through,* she thought, *or I am actual toast.*

*B*laring horns beeped in the background, driving nails into Bob's too-sensitive head.

Rolling gingerly to his side, he sat up in his bed and pressed the snooze on his alarm. His head throbbed.

I haven't had a headache like this since the war, he thought. *Wait,* his brain buzzed, *what war?*

Climbing out of bed, Bob vaguely registered that his arms were sore, as if he had torn muscles. *What did I do last night?* he wondered.

The smell of toast floated up to his nose and made him frown. *Who eats toast for breakfast?*

After carefully getting dressed, the man found his way into the kitchen, where Rose greeted him with a smile and then a confused double take.

"What are you wearing?" she asked with all the criticism a sixteen-year-old could muster.

"What's wrong with what I'm wearing?" Bob asked, looking down at his tailored button-down and light-gray slacks.

"I don't think I've ever seen you wear that. Like, not even when you had to meet Miss Henley after she threatened to suspend me."

Bob shrugged. "I found it in the back of my closet. Wait, why were you suspended?"

Rose huffed as she lambasted a piece of toast with cinnamon butter. "I wasn't! Stupid Matthew Hicks said I cheated off him because I wouldn't let *him* cheat off *me.* Why don't you remember that?"

Bob looked at the charred toast his daughter was making and licked his lips. He didn't want the unhealthy blob of sugars she held out to him anymore than he wanted his arms to continue aching. "I believe I'll have an omelet this morning," he announced, checking the fridge for eggs.

"Okay..." Rose said. "I guess I can eat this. Don't forget, Mom needs you to pick me up after practice and take me to her house tonight."

"Your mom?" Bob responded sluggishly.

"Yeah, Dad. She has a late meeting." Rose picked up her book bag. "Are you okay? You're acting really weird."

Bob shook his head and looked at his daughter. She had bright red hair, just like her mother. "Yeah, sorry, honey. I'll be there."

Rose stopped her mad dash to the front door and turned back to stare at her father. He had never called her "honey" before. It was a weird thing to just pick up.

Shrugging, she waved and shouted, "Love ya!" Then she ran out the front door.

Looking around his kitchen, Bob turned a knob on the stove to low before finding a large pan and placing it on the stove. He dropped a small scoop of salted butter into the slowly warming pan before grabbing a bowl and gently setting a fork beside it.

Finding eggs in the fridge, he carefully selected three from the carton before masterfully cracking them into the bowl one-handed. Adding a smidgen of water into the eggs, he beat them lightly until they were a creamy yellow, then poured them into the warm pan. Grabbing a rubber spatula, Bob stirred the eggs in a figure-eight pattern while adding a pinch of salt and pepper.

His mouth watered, while a little voice in the back of his head asked how in the seven hells he knew how to make a French omelet. Or that any decent French omelet contained a generous sprinkling of fresh chives—which he did not seem to have.

Bob started growing suspicious of himself as days went on. Whereas in the past, he tended to be messy and a little too carefree, now he seemed almost militarily organized, attentive, and generally kinder. His relationship with his ex-wife, Melissa, was much more cordial than it had been in years, and he had a newfound love of cooking.

Melissa danced around the topic until she finally asked him if he had started dating again. Rose confessed he was acting weird but promised she liked the changes in her father.

It's all well and good, he supposed, *but feeling like a stranger in your own skin is unsettling.*

"*Y*ou what?" asked Rose, a forkful of stuffed zucchini halfway to her mouth.

"I'm working at the Dalton as a sous-chef," Bob replied with a smile. "I started last week. I thought you and your mother would like to come by and enjoy a meal sometime soon."

Rose finished chewing before smiling and nodding. "That would be great! Could I bring Lauren? Her birthday is Thursday."

Bob chuckled. He'd been hoping for some quality time with Rose and her mother, but Lauren was a good influence. He'd opened his mouth to agree when a knock at the door caused him to jump up from the table.

"Expecting someone?" he asked with an arched brow.

Rose shoved another forkful of savory zucchini into her mouth and shook her head.

Peeping out the window, Bob couldn't help but frown at the man standing on the other side.

"May I help you?" Bob asked upon opening the door, not sure if he was supposed to know the fellow. He had suffered a few memory lapses lately, but so far, none of them had been people.

A somewhat stocky man dressed in a ridiculous beige raincoat looked up from under his fedora. He was wearing a wrinkled three-piece suit that was a gray sort of beige. A skinny black tie fell over a softening stomach, and a shoulder holster was just barely visible under his rumpled jacket.

"Robert Myers?" asked the man.

"Bob will do just fine," he replied, offering his hand for a shake.

"I'm Detective Ryan Parsons. I was hoping to ask you a few questions. Can I come in?"

Feeling defensive, Bob responded, "My daughter and I are having dinner, sir. May I inquire as to what this is regarding?"

Parsons looked startled by the respectful speech but simply slid a grin over his mouth. "Won't take long," he promised. "Just a few questions about November second."

Bob's lips popped open to form a small O before he nodded and stepped aside. That anyone save him might consider that date important seemed too coincidental. That was the night before he woke up craving omelets and experiencing holes in his memory. "Come in," he said, curious what this man would say.

"Dad?" Rose called from the kitchen.

Bob turned and smiled. "No reason for alarm, honey. Detective Parsons just needs to ask a few questions. You want to run upstairs and knock out the rest of your literature homework?"

Rose shrugged before shoving one final bite of food into her mouth. "Sure."

"No phone until it's done," Bob tossed over his shoulder as Rose ran upstairs.

"She's a good kid," he confessed to Parsons. "Just easily distracted."

Parsons nodded as if he agreed, but his gaze was taking in their surroundings. "Do you remember anything from that night?" he asked, starting his questioning without preamble. "November second?"

Bob shook his head. "Not that I can recall. Why is that date important?"

Parsons flashed another smile. "What about the following week or so? Anything stick out as different?"

"Different how?" The line of questioning was raising hairs on the back of Bob's neck. Why would anyone be interested in his life over the past few weeks? Sure, he had some memory glitches, but it wasn't negatively affecting anyone. Had Melissa hired this man? They had enjoyed joint custody of Rose over the last four years, but maybe Melissa wanted Rose full-time and this was a way to do it.

"Anything that might be a bit different than normal," Parsons prodded.

Bob shrugged. "I suppose not. I don't recall hearing or seeing anything out of the ordinary that night."

"What about personally?" asked Parsons, his gaze flitting around the entryway.

Bob shrugged again. "Typical midlife crisis, I guess," he said, smiling to cover his deception. "I took up cooking and organized my life a bit. I guess I decided to become a better person."

Parsons made a few notes, nodding the whole time.

"Anyway," Bob said and stood, an obvious dismissal. "Sorry I wasn't any help."

"No problem," Parsons said, placing his notepad back into his pocket. "I appreciate your time. Have a good night."

Later, when Bob turned his light off and slid into bed, he realized that Ryan Parsons had given no reason for being there.

"I don't get paid enough," grumbled Ryan Parsons as he tripped over the windowsill leading into Bob's sunroom and landed painfully on his knees.

Bob was at work and his daughter at school, so now was a great time to go poking around their empty house. He wasn't entirely sure why he was there, really. Most women were happy when their ex-husbands got their shit together. This lady, however, had hired him because Bob was becoming a better person. Parsons guessed that she was still in love with the guy and jealous that he may have found another woman.

She sounded like a nutcase, which made up at least half his clientele. The woman had actually brought a journal to his office and presented it as evidence of her ex's odd behavior.

"November third. That's the date Rose told me that Bob began acting strangely. He refused cinnamon toast for breakfast. Do you know how out of character that is?" Melissa had ranted at their meeting.

Not that he cared much either way. These domestic cases were boring and often lead him into situations like the one he was in now.

He sighed as he walked upstairs and made his way down the hall, looking for Bob's room. All he needed was a condom wrapper, or maybe a drawer full of women's clothing, to have enough to tell the ex-wife that Bob had moved on and she should too.

Finding Bob's room, Parsons inhaled deeply, looking for the scent of perfume, but smelled nothing. He popped his head into the bathroom and checked for an extra toothbrush or sanitary items, then frowned.

Bob would obviously be keeping this relationship from his daughter if his ex wasn't aware of it. So the girlfriend must visit on nights that Rose was with her mom, which meant no drawers or visible bathroom objects.

Stretching, Parsons lowered himself to the floor and peeked under Bob's bed. There were two clear containers of clothes, but not much else.

Damn.

As a last-ditch effort, the detective peeked behind the nightstand that butted up against a window. Not many people vacuumed under furniture if they had to move the curtains.

"Bingo." There was a strange gray-and-blue vial stuck behind the nightstand. He nabbed it and frowned. It looked like a large perfume bottle but had no smell.

"Good enough," he said, shrugging and wrapping his hand around the bottle.

Parsons's sight immediately faded to a blue-black haze, his head searing with an odd vision that played out like a movie. A woman in white stood before a group of horrifying beasts, speaking of a Master Plan and the spirits they would reap. The woman's voice was melodic, transfixing . . . and terrifying. He heard her give a count of the inevitable and unavoidable deaths for the week in a tone that almost suggested she was bored.

His brain felt like it was cracking with the weight of knowing his life and death were mapped out and nothing he did would change that.

The woman turned to stare directly at him before he felt himself being sucked back into his own reality.

"What the actual hell," he mumbled, his head pulsing like a strobe light. The woman's voice still echoed in his skull.

Pulling a handkerchief from his pocket, Parsons snatched the surprisingly weighty object and ran from the house as if it were collapsing behind him.

"I need a drink," Parsons muttered to himself. "Hell, I need three."

On autopilot, Parsons found himself at the Wiley Nickel, his bar of choice. The comforting notes of Muddy Waters welcomed the detective as he made his way to the back corner.

He liked to keep his back to the wall. It was an old habit that had saved his rear on enough occasions to make it worthwhile.

The stale smell of cigarette smoke mixed with the more pleasant one of spilled beer put him at ease, which had the unpleasant side effect of making him reflect on his life choices. He had given up smoking a time or two, but the smoke-sticks always won out in the end. Parsons's doctor had begged him to stop drinking, but he wasn't sure he wanted to live past the age of fifty anyway.

Settling back against his barstool, he held up two fingers to the barkeep—an older man named Jerry with salt-and-pepper hair and a five o'clock shadow that was probably closer to six o'clock.

The bar went to a lot of trouble to make itself seem like a prohibition saloon, and it pulled it off nicely. Jerry wore a blue button-down shirt with the sleeves rolled halfway up his forearms and a black bow tie that boasted picture-perfect diamond points.

The majority of the seating surrounded the wooden bar, which was a deep mahogany coated in a lacquer so perfectly smooth, it reflected like a mirror. Jerry kept the mirror shine up to snuff by constantly wiping the bar top. It was less about pride and more an attempt to keep his mind occupied despite the numbing boredom of his work.

Bottle-lined shelves were illuminated from above. Parsons noticed a new etched paddle hanging from the wall—a tradition the bar had to honor its barflies. Parsons's hung to the left of the bar, another reminder that he may be wasting his time.

Jerry reached for a rectangular brown bottle hidden behind the bar. Places like these typically tried to hide the gut rot in a speed tray as opposed to displaying it on one of the shelves. The bartender poured two fingers and brought the glass to Parsons.

"Detective." Jerry nodded as he set the glass on the bar.

Parsons rubbed his temples, trying to ease his headache. "Actually, I'll take the bottle," he said coarsely.

"That kinda night, eh?" inquired the well-dressed bartender.

"Every night is that kinda night," Parsons fired back, hoping to end the conversation before it began. He liked Jerry, but his head was threatening to split open.

Slamming back the double shot, Parsons had a flashback to his first year in the Army . . . and almost every night since then.

After a few shots, Parsons allowed his mind to wander.

What had he seen earlier? He had never paid much attention in school, but maybe he had had a stroke? It wasn't out of the realm of possibilities with the way he lived his life.

Emboldened by the false courage the alcohol had afforded him, Parsons decided to examine the perfume bottle he had pulled from Bob's house. He used his handkerchief to pull the gray bottle from his pocket and stared at it for a moment before he realized the blue markings around the bottle were not in English . . . or any alphabet he recognized.

Taking another shot, Parsons meandered over to a phone booth and punched in the ten digits that connected him to Bob's ex-wife.

"This is Melissa," she said by way of answering.

"This is Detective Ryan Parsons," he said, his voice velvety with whiskey.

"Oh, hello," Melissa said, somewhat uncertainly.

"Your ex-husband is seeing another woman. Nothing to be concerned about. He keeps nothing of hers in the house and has apparently kept her from Rose. I found a perfume bottle that had fallen down behind the nightstand. Men will do a lot to attract a mate," Ryan said, a small smirk creeping up his face. "That includes bettering themselves."

"I know it seems stupid to check up on an ex," Melissa stated, as if she were apologizing.

"You have your daughter to worry about," he said gallantly. "I understand."

As he made his way back to his whiskey, Parsons fumbled with the supposed perfume bottle again. It looked like an antique. He could sell the thing to the dealer off Clarke Street and make a few extra bucks from this witch hunt.

Without thinking, he caressed a finger over one of the glyphs. His headache intensified to the point of bursting. He was back in Bob's bedroom, the man's armless body floating in pools of blood. The lady in white was there again, standing next to a short wolfish man with too-dark eyes.

When Parsons came to, a few of the other patrons were side-eyeing him. He took one last shot, dropped a bundle of greenbacks on the counter, nodded his goodbye to Jerry, and half ran out the door. He needed to sleep this one off.

A bit shaky on his feet, Parsons took the shortcut down a back alley toward his apartment. He had the itchy feeling between his shoulder blades that made him think someone was staring at him from the shadows. Making a last-minute decision, he changed directions a few times to see if he could catch a glimpse of whoever was following him. Ryan knew it was fairly pointless, as drunk as he was, but his mind sorted down the list of people who might want to do him harm.

I paid my bookie off last week, so it can't be him. Could it be related to a case?

Feeling the hairs on his neck stand at attention, Ryan darted down a side alley and around a corner, his heart beating too rapidly. Sprinting to the entrance of the nearest building, he plowed through and up the stairs to the second floor. Pulling his sidearm, he peeked down the stairs from his vantage point but saw nothing except a dark, empty corridor.

Maybe I should give up drinking after all, he thought, shaking his head to clear his blurry vision. After a time, Ryan decided he was being ridiculous and stood from his crouch, looking around the building. Where the hell was he?

Backtracking the way he'd come, Ryan exited the building onto an alley he couldn't name. The moon was a quarter visible, shedding just enough light to turn the mist rolling off the street a nice shade of blue.

Wanting to get back to the main street, he headed back down the alley, noting the eerie silence. No street sounds at all. Not even a damn cat around to give him a jump scare.

The mist that had been slogging around his feet now thinned to the point where he could see a round cobblestone atrium connecting five alleyways. Gray concrete benches lined the circular opening, but Ryan's eyes were focused on the center, where an illuminated, radiant figure stood.

The woman in white.

*D*eath turned to face Ryan Parsons, her mouth pouting down at the edges in displeasure. She propped her hand on a thrust-out hip and tossed a lock of smooth hair over her shoulder.

"I believe you have something of mine," she said, her voice like honey pouring from the hive. "I need it back now."

If she got the vessel back, the Dreamers could tweak Parsons's memory, and she could be on her merry way. She hoped Max had enjoyed his time staring at his crush because she was fairly sure she was going to have the young monster's eyes plucked from his head. This business with Bob was causing too many hiccups in her schedule.

Teenagers, she thought with disdain.

"You're Bob's mistress?" Parsons asked, his jaw slack from apparent disbelief.

Death's pout raised at the corners, her eyes lighting up in mirth. "Years from now, maybe," she commented. "Give me the vessel, Ryan."

"Who are you?" Ryan demanded. "And how do you know my name?"

She shrugged, her sloped shoulders moving gracefully under her leather coat. "Death." She did enjoy the occasional dramatics, especially when they could be edited from memory.

"As in the Grim Reaper?" Ryan said stupidly. He paused for a brief moment before adding, "Where is your scythe?"

Death rolled her luminous eyes and clicked her tongue against her teeth. "God," she muttered. "You carry a scythe for a few hundred years, and no one lets you forget about it. It was a *phase*."

"You killed Bob?" Parsons asked, looking down at the vessel he had clutched in a handkerchief.

"Yes, and no. That was an unfortunate incident, really. It wasn't his time to go, so we resurrected him."

"You can't just *kill* people," Ryan said, taking a step forward.

"We *don't* kill them," Death said with an eye-roll. *Leave it to a man who's known about us for five minutes to think he has everything figured out.* "Souls are harvested at the point they leave their bodies. Consider us crows," she said, shifting her weight to her other hip. "If we did not harvest spirits after they left their bodies, they would settle like dust over the world, causing flashbacks like the ones you've experienced."

Ryan walked to one of the stone benches and flopped down. "Everything is preordained? So nothing we do means anything?"

Death's stiletto heels struck a cadence against the stone as she walked toward Ryan, sitting just to the right of him. "It's not all that bad," she consoled, patting his knee. "Human spirits fuel the Master Plan. Without you, there would be no balance in the world."

"Why are you telling me this?" Ryan asked, shifting his eyes to meet hers. "Are you going to kill me too?"

"Are you not listening?" she asked, her voice rising in displeasure. "We do not end lives, Ryan. We reap souls." Honestly, it wasn't a difficult concept.

"So you had to bring Bob back because he wasn't part of your Master Plan?"

Death smiled and nodded as if speaking to a child. "Exactly. His spirit was patched and reuploaded into his body… it's why he seems a bit off."

Ryan slumped forward, resting his head in his hands. His chest was tight with anxiety. If Bob could be a better man, than so could he.

"Patch me," he demanded. "Make me better. Do it, or I will go public with this."

"We were so close," Death lamented with an exaggerated sigh. "Wanting to be a better man should never be followed up with a threat," she chastised.

"You've already said you can't kill me," he said, his eyes widening. "You can patch me too. My life is a waste the way it is. If I'm slated to die at an appointed time, then at least let me be a better person until then."

She had to give it to the man, he wanted something more from his booze-fueled life. Technically, she could patch Parsons, but that would mean more people would find out that she had deviated from the Master Plan, not once, but twice.

If the Boss knew she was using resources to cover up her cover-up, she was toast. Burnt toast, at that. The irony of Death contemplating death was not lost on her, so she gave in to a rueful smile.

Retirement was being cut off from the spirit network, the Boss, and the Master Plan and scattered into the void. She would be sentient but unable to do anything save observe as the world ticked on endlessly before her. She wouldn't have to wear heels ever again, but being tormented with boredom over the span of eons sounded less fun than her stilettos.

Her contemplation was cut short by a quick movement to her left. Ember, an Envoy, stretched her orange furry hide and yawned. The fluffy thing seemed bored with their conversation, which should have been darkly humorous but just seemed dark considering the topic being discussed.

"What would you do differently?" Death asked the detective.

"With my life?"

She leaned back on the stone bench and nodded.

"I've wanted to start a security firm since I left the service," he said almost immediately. "And I should have married Sarah. She was the best thing I never knew I had. Don't suppose I did much good for her, but if I were a better person, it would work out."

This wasn't part of her job, but listening to the woes of mankind was centering. She had existed for ages, and they had mere moments.

Ryan suddenly spasmed and cried out, causing Death to startle at his side. The man fell to his knees in front of their shared bench, his knees thudding against the cobbled stone.

Ember padded over on all fours and sat near the detective, staring at a large tablet of scrolling text.

Death stared down at Ember. "What are you doing?"

Ember's fiery-red eyes went wide. The monster hesitated before showing Death the tablet she held in her right paw.

Detective Ryan Parsons

November 22 at 2:13 a.m.

Location: Five Points

Method: Heart attack

"Did I do something wrong?" Ember asked. Ryan clutched at his chest, his breath coming in shallow waves.

Death took a step toward the dying man, momentarily saddened for a reason she could not call to mind. Leaning over, she closed the man's bulging eyes and took the spirit vessel from his coat pocket.

"No, Ember. You did well."

All according to the Master Plan.

THE NIGHT SHIFT

Stephen Adams

It wasn't the easiest job, but it was the one that no one else wanted. I took it because I was tired of being cooped up on the inside. There are only so many weights you can lift and bad food you can eat before you start to go a little crazy. The work wasn't good and the pay was worse, but at least I got to breathe some fresh air.

The one good thing about the job was that the freedom felt great. They let me loose with the cleaning crew, and all I had to do was keep my nose clean, do the job, and show back up the next day in my cell. It was night work, so I could sleep during the day when all the other lowlifes were supposed to be up at breakfast and doing the normal routine.

My name's Roger, inmate #23895.

God, I loved the sound those gates made when they let me out. It was almost like being set free, except there was a white-panel van waiting for me. I didn't know what my first day was going to look like, but I knew it wasn't going to be glamorous. Warden Grayson had to meet with every one of us who wanted this job. As far as I knew, there were a couple of reasons for it. One was so they could decide whether we were a flight risk. I was too close to getting out to screw this gig up now. I was a lot of things, but I was no idiot. The second was to make sure we knew what we were getting into. The way they told it, it was like volunteering to get waterboarded for six hours. I'd been through worse. This job was about being on the outside, and that was all that really mattered to me.

I walked up to the white-panel van. The driver leaned over and rolled down the window. No power windows in this thing? How old was it?

"You're..." He trailed off as he flipped the pages on his clipboard. "Roger?"

"Yeah, that's me. You want me to ride up here, boss?" I was used to calling folks boss. It just felt like the best thing to say to keep from getting hit with a stick.

"Well, you ain't ridin' in the back. I got too much shit back there. Hop in."

I climbed into the van. There were old fast-food cups on the floor at my feet, and the dash had wadded-up pieces of paper everywhere. Most of them looked like receipts.

"This is a cleanin' company, isn't it?" I couldn't help myself.

"Smart-ass." The driver sounded gruff, but I could tell he liked the joke. "Buckle up, buttercup. It's gonna be a long night. You can still get out now, but the minute my foot sits on this pedal, you and I are in it together. Got it?"

"Yeah, whatever you say, boss. Let's go." I buckled my seat belt because, you know, it was the law.

"Suit yourself," he said, as he pulled the gearshift on the steering column and took us out on the road. "Name's Avery, by the way."

I looked at the back of the van as we headed toward the city. Bottles, rags, a couple of fifty-gallon drums, a few brooms, and some pump bottles were all tossed haphazardly around. For a cleaning company, these folks didn't seem to care so much for orderliness. I was starting to suspect that this might be some sort of ruse. Maybe population control for the inmates of America. Maybe this guy was just going to toss me in a barrel and melt me before dumping Roger-juice into the river.

"Hey, man. What is all this stuff?" I had to know. My imagination was starting to get carried away, and I didn't like the thought of myself in liquid form.

"That's the tools of the trade, my friend. What did they tell you about this job before they sent you out here with me? I'm guessing something about hazardous materials and cleaning up a mess? Nothing much else?"

"That's pretty much it."

"They might as well have been lying to ya. Thing is, the things we're cleaning up after ain't exactly..." He paused, searching for a word. "Well, they ain't like us."

This guy was a racist asshole.

"You're a racist asshole." I didn't hide my disdain.

"No, dumbass, not like that. Good God." He gained back a little bit of my respect, but not much. "I mean, they're monsters, kid. Like Oogie Boogie type. Hide-under-your-bed and steal-your-socks kinds of things."

Okay, he wasn't a racist. He was a lunatic.

"You're full of shit." I laughed, no longer trying to be the squeaky-clean inmate he might have wanted. I could tell a few swears weren't going to bother this guy. He looked like an old war vet. He'd seen things.

"Wish I was. Most people don't know anything about it, but a few of us lucky ones get to be gifted with the knowledge. At least, that's what they tell me every time I try to quit."

"Monsters?" I asked, still puzzled by the whole idea of things actually sneaking out of closets. And what the hell kind of monster steals socks?

"You said it. All kinds of different ones. Some of 'em even live around you and me. Shop at grocery stores, teach our kids at school, and make our drinks at our favorite bars. They're all right." He pulled a cigarette out of his front pocket and put it between his lips. He glanced at me. "You smoke?"

"Nah, been tryin' to quit."

"What for? Ain't like you got anything else to do."

That's what he thought. I was close to getting out, and I had some things to figure out before I got to walk back into my old life. "I got a girl on the outside who'd have a few things to say if I showed up still smokin'."

"Ah, you're the do-anything-for-a-woman type, eh? Yeah, I know you. Straighten yourself up on the inside, get outside, forget all the work you put in, and head back in for your three hots and a cot."

"I'm not goin' back."

"Do a good job tonight, and I might just believe you."

The city was getting bigger in the window as we drove up the highway. We were getting to the part of town with streetlights and sidewalks. Far from the rural outskirts that I had been calling home. It had been a long time since I'd been in the city. I still didn't quite believe this monster bullshit, but this quack could say whatever he wanted. I was on the outside and minutes from being able to set foot on pavement that my soles hadn't seen in years.

We pulled up to an apartment building on a nice side of town. Our van looked out of place with all the luxury cars parked on the street. A kid like me would have been up and down this street all night looking for some easy money, but this place was pretty lonely this late.

"First job is simple. Just clean. Grab a couple of those bottles with the X drawn on 'em and load 'em into the cart. I have some other essentials in my bag here." Avery got out of the van and wandered up to the door. He walked with a terrible limp. It was then I realized he had one leg shorter than the other. He was wearing one of those big boots that helped compensate for the difference. It worked well enough, but he was clearly still crippled.

I opened the back of the van and dug around for the stuff we needed. Everything was just out of reach, so I had to stretch over a bunch of the other barrels and bottles to get what I was after. Everything in the back smelled terrible. There was crust built up on the sides that looked like it may have been there for years.

As I was climbing out, I overheard Avery talking to someone at the door of the building.

"Yeah, we can handle it. We'll find the source of the smell, and you won't even know it was there." Avery flipped a paper over on his clipboard and handed it to the short balding man to sign.

"Thank you, Mr. Avery. She's not making it easy on any of us around here. The grandfather clause in this lease is really screwing me."

"You think she has a pet in there?"

"What else makes a smell this bad? I'm getting complaints from everyone in the building."

"Eh, no matter," Avery said. "Let's make this place livable. Roger!"

I pulled the cart around to the front steps of the building. Avery came down and helped me carry it up.

"Hello, sir," I said to the balding man.

He eyed me up and down. It didn't bother me much; I had gotten used to it.

"You signed up for a helluva job, sonny."

I hated being called sonny. My uncle used to call me that, and he was a pedophile. Not to me, but to someone. My whole family tree produced nothing but rotten apples. I shrugged it off and made my way into the building.

It wasn't a dump, but it wasn't immaculate either. There was a stench wafting around the place that made me almost want to lose my lunch. I'd never smelled anything like it before.

"Apartment we're cleaning is on the second floor. I'll grab this end of the cart, and you follow behind." Avery started making his way up the steps, and I followed suit.

"What's the job here?" I had to ask. If it was to fumigate the place, we needed more than a couple chemicals and a scrub brush.

"Clean it up. Get up there, open the door, evaluate, and then do the job. A lot of folks spend all their time wondering what they're gonna do. You and me, we're just gonna go up there and do whatever we have to. They pay me for it, and you get to be outside. Seems fair."

We made our way to the second floor, and Avery pushed open the door.

"Shit." That didn't make me feel any better.

"What is it?"

"Damn fuzzies."

"What?"

"Fuzzies!" he yelled, like it was going to help me understand what he was talking about.

"That's not helpin', man."

He started talking with his hands. "Little balls of fuzz. Little suckers have hands for feet and feet for hands. Damnedest thing you ever saw. Sharp little teeth too. Biters."

"What are we gonna do?"

"They're like bees, kid. They don't bother you if you don't bother them. Thing is, we have to clean up after the damn things. A lot worse than an average cat, I'll tell you that."

Avery reached into the cart and started putting on some gloves. I did the same. He was the pro around here.

"You smell that too, right?" I had been bothered by the stink since we walked in, but Avery seemed unfazed by it.

"Yeah. The smell is only gonna get worse. You can worry over it, or you can just understand it's there and deal with it. Come on." Avery started into the room and pulled the cart behind him. As I made my way in, the smell got worse.

"I hate these things," Avery said as he opened one of the bottles of chemicals. "They shit everywhere. Shit on the floor. Shit on the ceiling. Shit on the couch, drawers, sinks. Shit. Shit. Shit."

"Oh God, is that what all this dirt is?"

"Dirt." Avery chuckled to himself. I wasn't sure what was so funny. "Son, I have a feeling tonight is going to make you rethink your entire life experience. That's not dirt. It just looks like dirt. That, my friend, is fuzzy shit. Get that bottle, start spraying just all over any 'dirt' you think you see, and we have to sweep it into a bag. Stuff is like asbestos. You don't want it to get airborne." He pulled a couple masks out of his bag and tossed me one. "Safety first," he said, rolling his eyes.

I started digging through the cart for some bags. I put a few big black ones in my belt and sprayed the floor with the chemicals in the pump.

"Is this stuff gonna ruin their furniture?" I don't know why I was feeling so conscious over other people's things, but something about not wanting to lose this job was keeping me straight.

"Nah, but the fuzzy shit will. Stuff will seep into every crack in this place if you let it sit long enough. Good thing they called. Rick thinks she just has some big-ass dog in here."

We split up and started spraying all the surfaces in the apartment. This stuff was literally everywhere. They were lucky the building hadn't been quarantined and burned down.

"So where are these things, anyway? With this junk all over the house, I figured I would see one."

"You don't get to see just one of these if you see them. You get to see hundreds." Avery kept spraying. "You normals always think that monsters are some kind of huge damn thing. They come in all shapes and sizes. These little buggers are about the size of your toe. Like a caterpillar, but round. You ever seen that movie *Critters*?"

"The one where the little dudes with teeth turn into a giant ball and roll over a church?" There was literally one scene from that movie I remembered, but it seemed to get me all the traction I needed when it came to describing it.

"Yeah, that's the one. Those suckers were small, but they did a lot of damage. Imagine those, but instead of trying to eat everybody, they ate bugs and junk and then shit everywhere. That's what a fuzzy is. Enough talk. Let's get this job done and get out of here. We got more to do."

I felt like hours passed while we scraped up all the fuzzy shit. It was more brittle than I would have expected, falling apart just like a pile of dirt. Wetting it really was the trick to picking it up. Picking the stuff up dry would just get it sprinkled all over the place.

All that work, and I didn't see one damn fuzzy. The way Avery described them, I kind of wanted to put one in my pocket and get back to the cell with it. Maybe keep it as a pet. They let some inmates have a support animal. Something as small as a fuzzy I could probably keep and nobody would be the wiser.

As I was putting the last broom in the cart and Avery was doing a walk-through, I noticed a little brown fluff by the wheel. I looked over my shoulder to make sure Avery wasn't coming and knelt down to look at it. It was a small creature, no bigger than an average thumb. It looked like a little hedgehog, but it had tiny human feet near its head and tiny human hands at the bottom.

Feet for hands and hands for feet, I thought and smiled. "Come here, little guy," I whispered, as though this thing could understand me. When he got close enough, I picked him up. I may not have been the most sentimental person that ever lived, but I had a soft spot for animals. For some folks, it was all about the dog, but I would take a guinea pig. I put the little guy in my pocket just before Avery returned.

"That's it. Took longer than I wanted, but we got it done." He pointed at the bags with his pen. "Those have to be disposed of back at the shop. We'll throw 'em in the back and roll the windows down. Should be fine. Grab the cart, and let's ship out. Night is young."

"Sure, boss." I grabbed the back end of the cart, content with my decision to steal a tiny monster from this apartment. I wasn't even considering the trouble that something so small could cause.

We loaded everything back into the van and slammed the back doors shut. I was only slightly unnerved that there was an entire world of creatures I'd never seen before and that I was just now figuring it out. I had always imagined monsters in my closet or hiding under the bed, but once I got old enough, I didn't believe in them. This work release job was turning me into less of a skeptic. I supposed that was a good thing, but I didn't have enough evidence to be sure.

"Quit your daydreaming and get in the van, kid," Avery yelled, bringing me out of my haze.

Before I got within his sights, I checked on the little thing in my pocket. It was kind of like carrying around a funny-looking gerbil. He didn't make any noise, so it wasn't too hard to keep him hidden from Avery. I opened the passenger door and climbed back in.

"Where we headed next?" I asked, looking forward to the next job.

"We're going to see Maxwell," Avery replied, putting the clipboard on the dash. "He's a regular. Calls every now and then when he needs something. Good tipper, so don't stare, do the job well, and you might walk out with some extra cash." He paused for a moment. "I mean, I'll come out with extra cash. They don't let you folks take much home. That bein' said, make a good impression, and I'll make sure the powers that be know you did me a solid."

"You got it, boss. Whatever you say," I said, like the little lapdog I was meant to be. I really couldn't wait to get back on the outside on my own. Sucking up to every guy in a suit, even a white jumpsuit, was getting to be too much. You stay subservient long enough, and you start to believe you're not worth the meat it took to put you together.

We drove south toward a rougher part of town. To be honest, I was starting to feel more comfortable the farther we got from the fancy cars and nice townhouses. It was nice to gawk at how the other half lived, but I don't envy those people. I had the stress of making sure no one shanked me on a daily basis, but these folks had taxes, mortgages, divorces, children, and stepchildren. To be fair, no one was out to shank me anyway. I got a roof over my head and edible food. That was enough to keep me from trying to climb the walls. I was ready to go insane with boredom some days, but that was what this job was supposed to fix. If I kept it up, they might just let me stay on.

We pulled up to a nice-enough-looking house with a front porch swing. It was one of those old colonial-style deals with steps up to a front porch and a big front door. It wasn't anything special and it needed some love, but overall I'd live in it.

Made me think that once I got on the outside, I might be able to make a few bucks fixing up houses or doing simple renovations. Hell, if this worked out, I could clean up after monsters, I guess. I didn't know it was a thing less than six hours ago, but I was starting to think I could create a career out of it.

"All right, kid. I got two rules," Avery said, raising two fingers and staring daggers through me. "No staring and no unnecessary questions. This guy, Maxwell, he's not like you and me. This guy is something else. He's kind of a weirdo, but you and I have to act like he's a normal, everyday guy."

We got out of the van and went to the door. The steps of the porch creaked as we walked up. Avery knocked on the door and looked at me. "Remember what I said, kid."

The door swung open, and standing there was a completely average-looking guy. After Avery's pep talk, I thought I'd be looking at some dude with four eyes and tentacle hair, but this was actually a well-put-together man. He was dressed incredibly well. He wore a blue, three-piece pinstripe suit and wing-tip shoes. His graying hair was a bit disheveled, but in a trendy way. His face was pale with sunken dark eyes. He looked like he could use some sleep.

"Avery, thank God," the man said before glancing harshly at me and pointing his finger. "Who's this?"

"Rookie. Don't worry over him. What can we do for you?" I was learning that Avery didn't bother with niceties. Suited me fine. I was never good at them anyway.

"I had another..." He paused, looking at me suspiciously. "Accident."

"Drifter? Bum? Talk to me, Maxwell."

"It's difficult to tell. I didn't find a wallet or any identification. It looks like he wasn't carrying anything of any particular value." Maxwell started to tear up a bit. "Oh God, it's so awful. I can barely stomach even going in the room."

"Pull it together. We'll get it taken care of." Avery was so deadpan in his delivery. He clearly had been in this game long enough that very little ever surprised him.

I was still trying to process. I liked to think of myself as resilient. A person don't grow up like I did and not come out with a strong wit and an even stronger stomach.

"It's in my basement. I'm not sure how or why, but it seems that I can control at least some of my, um... impulses. Please come in."

"Kid, go to the van and get our stuff. You'll find a white canister with a red top. There's a powder in it. We'll also need the blue bucket, the bag of rags, and a couple brooms. Don't spill anything, and if you can't get it all, take two trips."

Avery reminded me of my dad. He used to give me specific instructions like that—when he was around anyway. Not because I was dumb or anything, but because he thought I might be. Avery had a slight no-nonsense way about him, but it wasn't unkind. My dad had been different. Same words, completely different person behind them and a completely different feeling. I had a feeling Avery wasn't planning to hit me if I messed up, but I didn't intend to find out.

Avery entered the house with Maxwell. I could tell Maxwell was still eyeballing me from the porch as they turned to go inside. Not sure what I'd done to make him not trust me, but something told me he don't get out much. I walked over to the van and swung the doors open. Gathering the supplies, I figured a good way to get everything in one trip. I put the containers in a couple five-gallon buckets, put the brooms through the handles, and created a shoulder harness. Getting a job done quick meant more yard time. More yard time meant more sun, and I needed the sun. Before heading inside, I looked in my shirt pocket at the fuzzy. He looked back up at me with his little hedgehog face. He was a cute little guy. A bunch of these could sure make a mess, but how much harm could one really do?

I gathered up my stuff and went inside the house. It was incredibly well kept. Nothing looked out of place. There was a fire crackling in the living room, dark wood paneling on the walls, and beautiful rugs covered the hardwood floors. I felt like I had just walked through a time warp. I didn't see a TV, and there was a rotary phone on the table in the foyer.

"Hello!" I yelled through the house.

"Down here!" came Avery's gruff voice in reply.

I walked toward the slightly open door at the end of the hallway. It led to some steps that turned ninety degrees about two-thirds of the way down, so I couldn't quite see where everyone was. Getting down the steps with my broom-handle rigging was a bit harder since I had to turn sideways and try to keep everything level. I was proud of all the lifting I had done, that's for sure.

"Hope you have a strong stomach, kid," Avery said with a sense of dread in his voice.

I turned the corner, and for a moment, I thought the room had been painted red. There was blood everywhere. The space itself was more like a garage. It had a hard concrete floor and cinder block walls, with flickering fluorescent lights hanging from above. I couldn't have been more creeped out. I turned my head and held back my dinner. This was a lot worse than the fuzzy shit.

"You all right?" Avery asked, seemingly more out of obligation than concern.

"Yeah, boss, I'm good," I lied. Truth be told, this was going to be a struggle, and for the first time tonight, I questioned my decision to sign on for this job.

"You must forgive me," Maxwell chimed in. "I'm not sure what came over me. One moment, I'm sitting in my chair, reading a wonderful book; the next, I'm naked and covered in . . ." He paused. "Someone. These occurrences have become increasingly rare, but they do happen nonetheless."

"We'll get it taken care of. No one will know." Avery said without look up from the mess we were soon to tackle. "Anyone important?"

"Not that I can tell. As I said, I was unable to find identification, and the scraps of clothing that were here seemed dirty and not well taken care of. I have already put them in the waste bin. If I had to guess, he was a drifter." Maxwell looked at me as though it were almost a guarantee his words offended me. They hadn't. "Though there is nothing wrong with such a lifestyle. We all should enjoy a bit of freedom, shouldn't we?"

He smiled at me, and for the first time, I noticed his sharp teeth. Like a shark smiling before it takes a bite out of its prey. I must have looked shocked because he quickly closed his lips. He glared at me, losing much of the friendly countenance that I had come to know up to this point.

"Why does he look at me like that, Avery?" he asked, not taking his eyes off me.

"What?" Avery tried to not look horrified, but it was barely working. "Oh, he's got some screws loose. Just another kid from the prison. They don't get out much." He quickly steered the subject back to the task at hand. "You go on upstairs and get yourself a cup o' tea or whatever and relax. We'll be done in about an hour or so."

Avery shook his head at me as Maxwell turned to go up the stairs. As soon as our host was out of earshot, he lit into me. "What the hell, kid? I gave you two rules, and you've already pissed him off. Do you *want* to die tonight? Good God." He turned, shaking his head, and began assessing the room.

"Sorry, boss," I said. "It won't happen again."

"You're damn right it won't. It happens one more time, and you won't have eyes left to stare with. Give me that white bottle, and let's get this done so we can get out of here."

I passed him the white bottle of powder. He opened it up and started sprinkling it all over the walls and floor, wherever there were red stains. "Good thing about Maxwell is, he knows what he is. He knows what he can do. He also has trained himself to only make messes in this room. Not all of them work this way."

"What does he do, anyway?" I had to ask. It was killing me.

Avery looked past me, as if to ensure Maxwell still couldn't hear us. "He's a wolfman."

"Wait, like a werewolf?"

"Nah, they don't like that word. Truth is, they don't like *wolfman* either, but that's what we call them. Maxwell is a good one. Most of them are like barbarians. They think they're better than us and love picking us off. Maxwell couldn't stomach the idea. Never joined a pack."

I was still stuck on the idea that there was a real live werewolf upstairs, sipping tea and reading a book. "Like a full-moon, silver-bullet, transforming werewolf?"

"Yeah, kid," He sounded a little irritated with me. "But it ain't like the movies. All that full moon stuff is bullshit. They can turn anytime.

If they're angry, upset, anxious, or scared. You know, 'fight or flight.' These just fight, and they win."

"Damn," I said, trying to figure out how to process all this new info. The fuzzies were one thing, but an honest-to-God werewolf was another.

"Yeah," Avery agreed. "Now get your stuff and start sweeping up this junk."

I hadn't been paying much attention while Avery was sprinkling the powder. Had I been, I would have noticed that it was sucking up all the blood. The white powder was turning red, but it stayed sort of fluffy. I swept a bit of it, and it looked spotless underneath.

"Man, this stuff works great," I said as I continued.

"Can't buy it anywhere, so don't get to thinkin' you're gonna have a career hocking cleaning stuff when you get out of the clink. Shop has a chemist that makes this stuff. Real creepy joker. Won't tell anyone what he uses, but I don't care. Paycheck clears."

We sprinkled and swept for the next hour, until we finally got all the blood up. I didn't know what Maxwell did with the rest of the body, but my guess was that we didn't need or want to know.

"Pack it up, kid," Avery said. "I'll get Maxwell's signature, and you get our junk in the van. We got time for one more run."

"Sure thing, boss." I gathered up our stuff in the buckets. Looking at the work we'd done, I couldn't help but feel proud. I also couldn't help but feel a cleaning company like this could erase almost every crime in the city if they chose. There wasn't an ounce of blood in the room and no way anyone would be able to tell that something horrible had happened there. I wondered how many times I'd been in a place that these folks had visited. How much death were we surrounded by at all times and never had a clue?

I made my way up the stairs and into the hallway when I smelled it. Something disgusting had made its way into my nose, and I had no idea where it was coming from. I almost fainted, it hit me so hard. It was like walking into the world's worst bathroom.

The fuzzy.

I looked in my pocket, and this cute little hamster of a monster had dropped an enormous amount of shit. It was at least the size of him. My shirt pocket was filled almost one-third of the way, and the little guy was just sitting in it. Not only was it a huge amount of shit, but it smelled like it. I walked up the hallway, past an opening to what looked like the kitchen. Maxwell was sitting at a small table with Avery, filling out some paperwork. Both of them looked up, and I could tell Maxwell was sniffing.

"What . . . ?" He paused. "What is that smell?"

"Ah, that's nothing. Chemical residue, Maxwell. Sign the paper, and we'll be on our way." Avery looked at me. I could tell he wasn't okay. It was the face of someone disappointed and terrified at the same time.

He knew.

"Good lord." Maxwell was starting to shake. "Is that you?" He looked directly at me, his eyes twitching.

"Yeah, yeah, I'm leaving," I said, unsure what else to say.

"You have a fuzzy in your pocket." His voice was deep. The statement rattled as it came out. He snorted. "You brought that filth into my beautiful home?" His shaking grew worse. "With its EXCRE-MENT?" He was shouting now. His eyes turned red.

Avery jumped up and grabbed the paper. "Go, kid. Now!" He ran out the doorway and hurried down the hallway.

I waddled quickly behind him with the buckets and broom handles over my shoulders. I was not as quick as I needed to be. Behind me, I could hear a bloodcurdling scream and a horrible cracking sound. I turned to look.

Crawling through the doorway was something that barely resembled Maxwell. It was a bleeding mess of an upper body. His face contorted into a dog's muzzle, wrinkled and bloody. The bones in his face rearranged with a sickening pop. The suit that Maxwell had been wearing was ripped at the shoulders as he grew.

Avery hurled the door open and ushered me out. "God, kid, move! Lose the buckets! We don't have time!"

I dropped the buckets and ran the next ten feet to the door. I couldn't look back, but I could hear the stomping behind me. It increased in frequency and grew heavier with each step. I ran out the front door. As I looked back, Avery pulled the door shut hard, just before the hulking beast got to him. He reached up above the door-frame and pulled down a huge metal roll-up door. As it hit the door-frame at the bottom, it latched. Immediately after I heard the click of the latch, the pounding began. Maxwell was coming.

"Lose the shirt. Get in the truck!" Avery yelled as he hurried down the steps after me. I pulled the shirt over my head, trying not to get fuzzy shit on me while I did. The little guy was still in there, but it was either him or me, and today it was definitely not going to be me. I threw the shirt in the bushes by the sidewalk and jumped in the passenger seat. Avery cranked up the van and floored it, throwing me back into the seat. The look of this old white van was misleading. I think we went from zero to sixty in six seconds. I'd never been in a car so fast.

I looked in the mirror and was able to see the shadow of a beast and the torn-up metal front door. The beast was sniffing through the bushes. *So long, little guy.*

"What in the seven hells were you thinking?" Avery spoke up after a long silence. "We have one job, kid. Clean up shit. We go in, we do a job, we leave. We don't take souvenirs, we don't make friends, we don't judge. We clean up. We leave. That's the deal. We're the only reason you didn't know about monsters until today."

"I just thought I could keep the little guy as a pet. I didn't know we'd be going to the house of a werewolf who just happened to love the smell of fuzzy shit." I was being more combative than I had so far. The number one rule of a work release was to keep your mouth shut and do what you're told. But if there was one thing I was good at, it was breaking the rules.

"I don't have to tell you every damn thing, kid. I have to tell you what will keep you alive. If you didn't have that damn thing in your pocket, Maxwell would still have a front door. If we're lucky, he finds it and goes back inside to roll around in his self-pity some more. If we're unlucky, we get called back tomorrow to pick up somebody else's pieces. You think about that."

It hit me then that all I had done back there was hide a criminal. Nobody had ever done that for me, and the idea of it was pissing me off. "Why the hell do we help monsters, boss? If I murder someone, I go to jail. Hell, I ripped off a gas station, and I'm in jail. I just helped clean up a crime scene, and that guy gets to go free. How's that fair?"

It just hit me that all I did back there was hide a criminal. Nobody did that for me and the idea of it was pissing me off.

"Life's not fair, kid. Least of all for them. You think any of 'em asked for what they got? They just got dealt a shitty hand. You made choices to get here. You're riding in this van with me because you made a bad decision and got locked up. Maxwell back there? He didn't choose to eat somebody. It chose him, and he gets to live with it every damn day."

"You're not wrong. I made a bad move; that's the truth," I said, finally coming down off my little tantrum. "Why do we protect them, though? If they're out there killin' people, why aren't we defending ourselves and killin' them? Why help them hide?"

Avery sighed. "They ain't the bad ones."

"What does that even mean?" I asked, fairly certain I'd just cleaned up a dead person from the basement of a werewolf who then tried to eat me.

Avery was quiet for a bit. "You see a spider in your house, right?"

"Okay, yeah."

"What do you do to it?"

"I smash it with a shoe or something." I didn't even have to think about it.

"What if you took the spider and put it outside?"

I looked at him, having no idea where this was supposed to be going. "I don't know. I guess it would wander off."

"Sure, the spider would wander off. Probably go about its little spider life, catching bugs, building nice webs, having little spider babies. It probably would never bother you again."

"Yeah, but I don't know what this has to do with monsters eatin' real people."

"Let's say you squash the spider. Maybe this spider knows some people. Maybe this spider has a huge family. Maybe it's part of a giant network of other spiders, and these guys don't play around. They find a way into your house. They build huge webs. They wait until you're sleeping, and they suck you dry." Avery looked at me for a moment.

"You don't know monsters exist because we make sure you don't. If we ran out there with our pitchforks in hand, trying to kill all of 'em, what do you think would happen? You think they would all just go away? Nah, they would go into hiding, they would grow in number, and they would turn around and we'd be gone. People tried fighting them for years, and it wasn't good for us. We made a truce, and now we watch out for 'em so people don't freak out and start slinging bombs. We're going on five hundred years of peace, and my job is to make sure that lasts."

"What happens if we give them a chance to get us first, though? What if Maxwell decides he's tired of hidin', runs out of his house, and eats half of Manhattan? We have all kinds of monster-killing shit. The way I see it right now, that werewolf could eat me, my friends, whoever, while they was walking down the street minding their business. The fuzzies were just little hamster shit factories, but that guy back there? He's a real threat. We oughta deal with them when we find them. Slip into the house and take them out while they're asleep, or something."

"Maybe. But what would that make us?"

I thought about that for a bit.

If there was one thing I had in prison, it was time. Time to think about all the decisions I had made or would make. Time to figure out if I was a good person who screwed up or a bad person who actually belonged in there. Maybe that was what Maxwell was. A guy locked in a prison trying to keep from being the bad person he knew he was.

"Here." Avery finally broke the silence and tossed his clipboard at me. "What's our next job?"

I flipped the paper on the clipboard and read it over. *Damn,* I thought.

MURDER CLEANUP: MONSTER VICTIM—DEMONKIN

ADDRESS: 1000 ROOTS WAY—BACK ALLEY

Detail: Need body disposal + scene cleanup. Adolescent monster. Unarmed. Next of kin notified. Requires typical discretion.

MPD Report: suspect hunter. Victim killed in cold blood for sport. No evidence to show otherwise.

Neither of us said anything. I had started this job believing that there were no monsters. After tonight, I didn't know what being one meant anymore.

*E*ric was at the chalkboard, nervously trying to figure out the value of x in front of the whole class, when the Visitation Alarm rang out, announcing the coming of a god.

He automatically dropped the chalk, covered his eyes, and flopped down to bury his head in his knees as Mrs. Vance bolted to the front of the room and took control.

"Heads down, everyone!" she commanded in her do-*not*-disobey-me tone. "Heads down and eyes closed this instant!"

The seventeen eighth graders in her care were quick to comply. Though as rowdy and rambunctious as any group of thirteen-year-olds, none of them even considered sneaking a peek through their fingers or hair. Nobody ever ignored a Visitation Alarm. In just a few seconds, the class transformed from a disorganized cohort of bored kids, jeering at their fellow classmate's struggles at the chalkboard, to a focused unit of penitent, obedient children, ready for worship.

"Who would like to begin the Recitation of Humility?" asked Mrs. Vance, her voice slightly obscured as she sat at her desk and covered her head with her arms. "Eric? Why don't you start?"

Eric rolled his eyes. It was safe to do so since his head was covered and no one would see. He parroted the words that were drilled into every child's head from birth. "We give thanks and praise to the wise and powerful ones for deeming humanity worthy of survival," he began. "As lower forms of life, we accept we are cosmically insignificant. We thank you, our gods, for allowing us the opportunity to forever strive to improve our race."

"Very good, Eric," came Mrs. Vance's muffled praise. "Jessica? Please continue."

"Our defects are disappointingly many," piped up Jessica, a total teacher's pet. "One, that our minds fail to grasp the absolute infinite. Two, that our bodies are weak and fragile. Three . . ."

Eric checked out as Jessica prattled on with all the ways humans were inferior to the gods. He wondered if the Visitation would last long enough to get him out of his torture at the chalkboard. He was actually pretty good at math and probably could have done the problem alone at his desk. But in front of the class, with everyone staring? Not a chance. And as his classmates had sensed his obvious discomfort, they had sunk their teeth into him with sneers and giggles. True, the jeers were under their breath and probably not meant for his ears, but the curse of his excellent hearing picked up every whispered taunt aimed his way, turning the uncomfortably difficult task into a hopelessly impossible one.

Suddenly, the whole world shook as a deep, deafening boom reverberated against the walls from outside and the sound of shattering glass filled the room.

"Heads down, children!" shouted Mrs. Vance. "Keep your heads down! It sounds as though we are being blessed with an especially close Visitation today!"

A second after she said it, the whole class could smell that it was true. A soggy, rotten, metallic stench floated in through what Eric supposed was a broken window or two. In the back of his mind, he wondered if being up in front of the class struggling with multiplication had just saved him from getting peppered with shards of glass, seeing how his seat was next to the windows and all. The foul air caused a couple of kids to cough, and it sounded to Eric like one of the coughs was a little wet, so maybe someone had puked. He hoped it was Arnold; that kid was a jerk.

"We should sing! Children, this is a perfect time to sing your Hallelujahs and show your faith!"

Mrs. Vance's quavering voice began the repetitive chorus of "Hallelujah, Gods of Old! Hallelujah, Gods of Now!" and one by one the children joined in as best they could. They stumbled a bit during the naming verses (Hallelujah Tsathoggua! Hallelujah Azathoth! etc.) but came back in with feeling on the chorus.

Eric, who had always liked singing the Hallelujahs as they were great tongue twisters, joined in with gusto. But just when he'd wrapped his vocal cords around 'Hallelujah Shub-Niggurath!' a piercing scream ruptured the room's mounting religious fervor, along with a sickly squelching noise and a truly repugnant odor that brought tears to Eric's eyes. Eric couldn't immediately identify the screamer, but it was definitely one of his classmates. Whoever it was, their scream proved infectious because pretty soon just about everyone in the classroom was screaming, while Mrs. Vance did her best to layer her voice on top.

"Stay calm!" she cried. "Do not open your eyes! Do not look at the god!"

As crazed as the room was, she needn't have worried. Nobody in their right mind would dare lift their head before the Visitation's End Klaxon rang out, not unless they wanted their eyes to melt out of their skulls.

The earth quaked once again, though not as strongly as before. The smell became slightly less horrifying. The god was moving on. In the stillness that followed, Eric heard a number of his fellow classmates sniffle and whimper, but his mind was dwelling on a different sound. One he'd heard, or thought he'd heard, right after the first kid screamed.

The Visitation's End Klaxon finally rang true, and everyone lifted their heads and gasped. The entire wall of windows had shattered, and three of the four kids with desks by the windows were bleeding from multiple scrapes, though none of the cuts looked all that deep. But that wasn't what made everyone gasp.

"Jimmy's gone!" yelled Hannah, staring at the empty seat directly in front of her.

Mrs. Vance quickly jumped up from her chair and ran forward. "A miracle!" she said. "He's Ascended! Children, one of your own classmates was deemed worthy by the gods of Ascension! Hallelujah! Praise the gods! Sing! Everyone sing!"

The stunned students were slow to add their voices to Mrs. Vance's in celebration. None of them had ever witnessed a Holy Ascension before, and to be this close to such a divine moment had put them all at a loss for words.

Eric, whose glass-covered seat was next to Jimmy's, was also at a loss for words, but not necessarily due to the sanctity of the moment. He was still mulling over the sound his highly acute ears had made out at the end of Jimmy's scream.

It had been a very disturbing sound.

*E*ric sat with his family around the dinner table, the disturbing details of the day's event swirling through his mind.

"Mmm! These are great . . . *potatoes!*"

His little sister, Bonnie, beamed with the thrill of the family secret.

"I'm glad you like them, Bonnie," their father said with a wink.

Eric ignored the show and cut into the contraband sirloin on the plate in front of him. Legally, meat was for the gods, and the gods alone. However, Eric's father worked in one of the slaughterhouses and would occasionally smuggle home a roast or chicken breast for his family. His supervisors knew, of course, but they looked the other way, as they generally did for all their employees. The only requirement was that nobody mention the fact they were eating meat out loud. Hence, Bonnie's excessive exuberance for what she loved to call potatoes.

"I really love . . . *potato* . . . night!"

"That's enough, honey," said their mother. "Please take another bite."

"Of my . . . *potato?*"

"Gods, Bonnie, will you shut up and eat already?" snapped Eric.

The precocious seven-year-old glared at her brother, who glared right back.

"Your brother's right, hon," said Dad, picking up a piece of celery from his plate. "Even if he could stand to be a little more considerate with his choice of words."

Dad popped the celery in his mouth and chomped down. The sound sent a shiver through Eric's body.

"And how was your day, Eric?" asked Mom, deftly trying to change the subject. He could tell by her tone she was ignorant of the day's events. That meant the school hadn't made any calls yet, which was just as well. He was still pretty shaken up and didn't feel like talking about it.

"Fine," he mumbled in between bites of illegal steak.

"More than fine, I'd say," remarked Dad, still crunching his celery. "Mrs. Vance told me you had a serious, up-close-and-personal Visitation at school today."

Mom gasped. Bonnie dropped her fork. Eric sighed.

"Really?" asked Bonnie. "You saw a god?"

"Don't be stupid," snapped Eric. "I still have eyes, don't I?"

"She said James Galloway Ascended," continued Dad.

"What?" screeched Bonnie. "Lucky!"

Mom shot a glance at Dad, then looked away.

"That must have been pretty amazing," finished Dad. "A real spiritual moment, eh?"

"Yeah, I guess," responded Eric. He dragged his fork absently around his plate, suddenly not very hungry.

"Did you sing your Hallelujahs?" asked Mom. "I know how you love those."

"Yeah, we sang," said Eric, silently adding, *right until Jimmy started screaming in terror.*

"Did Jimmy say anything before he Ascended?" asked Bonnie.

"It doesn't work like that," Eric said. "He was just sort of gone. Which actually kind of sucks because we were gonna go over to his house after school and play Mortal Murder on his Playgo game console."

"I think an individual's spiritual Ascension is more important than playing a video game," chastised Mom.

"Whatever."

Mom and Dad shared another look. Eric couldn't decide if they thought they were being covert or if they just didn't care if their kids saw them.

"How are you doing with all this?" asked Dad. "You must have questions."

Questions? Yeah, he had questions. But he doubted his folks wanted to hear them.

Luckily, Bonnie was more than happy to ask questions in his stead.

"How do you get chosen to Ascend? Do you just need to be good for a long time? I don't remember Jimmy being a good kid. He pulled my hair the last time he was at our house."

"It's a combination of things, honey," said Mom. "We can't ever know what the gods are looking for or why they choose to allow one person to Ascend over another."

"But being good has something to do with it, right? Do you need to learn all the Hallelujahs? Because I'm trying, but I sometimes get Nyarlathotep and Nyctelios mixed up. And I can never pronounce Czack . . . Cksackoo . . ."

"Cxaxukluth," prompted Dad.

"Right, see? Do I need to get that right to Ascend?"

It was too much for Eric, who finally blew up. "Oh gods, will you shut up!" he cried. "It's all a damn lie!"

"Eric!" shouted Dad.

"There's no such thing as Ascension, okay?" Eric continued, finally giving voice to the nagging doubt that had first hooked its talons in his gut when he'd heard his friend scream for his life. "Just forget about it!"

"Don't be absurd, Eric," chided Dad, awkwardly glancing about the room. "You saw Holy Ascension take place before your very eyes just this afternoon."

"Of course I didn't, Dad! My head was buried in my knees. I didn't see anything! But I heard, Dad! I heard Jimmy scream out in terror, heard him scream for mercy, heard him scream bloody murder!"

"Ascension is such an emotional moment, Eric. People can't control themselves," explained Mom hurriedly. "Screaming is very common when someone is lifted up to be with the gods."

"You weren't there, Mom! I'm telling you, Jimmy wasn't gently lifted up anywhere. In fact . . ." Eric paused, knowing full well the effect his next words would have on his family. But he didn't care. "In fact, I think he was eaten."

"What!" screamed Bonnie, eyes wide in shock.

"No! Absolutely not!" Dad was up on his feet, his face red. "That's absurd blasphemy!"

"Eric, you know that isn't true," added Mom, still in her seat but equally upset.

"I heard it!" pressed Eric. "I heard his bones being crunched and cracked, heard the slobber of some massive thing chewing—"

"Stop!" shouted Dad. He held his palm out as if he could force his son's mouth closed by force of will. "Don't say that!"

"He was eaten?" asked Bonnie, lips trembling.

"Of course not, honey," soothed Mom, staring not at Bonnie but up at the ceiling. "Eric's just confused."

"I'm not confused!"

"Sandra, take Bonnie upstairs," commanded Dad. "Now."

If Mom had a problem with her husband ordering her about, she didn't show it. She rose to her feet and grabbed her daughter by the arm. "Come with me, honey."

"Did something eat Jimmy?" Bonnie asked again.

"No, Bonnie Baby," said Mom hurriedly. "Jimmy Ascended. Your brother's just feeling the guilt of the Overlooked. It's perfectly natural."

"Why are you lying to her? You know that's a crock!"

"Sandra!"

Mom tugged Bonnie up the stairs. "Come, honey."

"What is wrong with you people?" asked Eric, venting at his father while the man watched his wife and daughter disappear up the stairs. "I'm telling you what I heard! Something sick and disgusting and evil yanked my friend out of his seat and ate him! Are you even listening to me?"

The instant the women were out of sight, Dad whirled around and slapped Eric in the face, stunning him into silence.

"Shut up! Just shut up!" roared Dad.

Eric stepped back upon seeing the look in his father's eyes. Unexpectedly, it wasn't anger or rage, but fear.

"I don't care what you think you heard. Jimmy Ascended. It was a wonderful spiritual moment. A blessing from the benevolent gods that roam our world."

"Benevolent? The thing smashed through the wall of my school!"

"A wall that the council just recently decided was unsafe. They wanted to tear it down and build a safer one but couldn't afford the demolition. Now they have been spared that expense. Hallelujah! Praise the wisdom of the gods!" Dad's final exaltation was directed up at the ceiling.

"Oh, come on!"

"You're confused. I understand. But it'll pass. Do you hear me? It'll pass!" Eric suddenly got the weird feeling he wasn't the only one his father was addressing. "You need to go upstairs and pray. Pray for acceptance of Jimmy's Ascension. Pray for forgiveness for questioning the gods. It'll all make sense in the morning."

Dad leaned forward and grabbed Eric by the shoulders, drawing him in close and staring into his eyes. "Say it with me, Eric. It'll all be better in the morning."

"Dad, you're creeping me out—"

"Say it!"

"Okay! Okay! I'm totally wrong. It'll be better in the morning! Happy?"

Dad maintained the too-close connection between them for a moment, then lifted his head around, as if looking up into the corners of the ceiling. "Good. Good," he said finally, letting go of Eric's shoulders. "Good. You go pray. Pray to whichever god you want. Who's your favorite? Cthulhu, right? You've always liked Cthulhu. Pray to Cthulhu. Go on."

He stepped away and smiled. Eric frowned. His father's smile was just as forced as Eric's fake mea culpa had been.

"Go on, Eric. Go pray."

"Yeah. Whatever," said Eric. He brushed past his father and trudged up the stairs to his room.

They came for him that night.

He was standing in the middle of an empty classroom. Not his, but larger and ringed on all sides by floor-to-ceiling windows. The desks were lined up neatly in rows but coated with a thick layer of blood. And something else. A nasty, fetid slime oozed and bubbled up from the floor.

Jimmy was there, standing in the corner. Then he was standing right in front of Eric, who could see that his friend's eyes had popped out of their sockets and hung down, dangling from yellow-purple veins and bouncing around like broken Slinkys.

"Jimmy . . . what . . . where . . ."

Jimmy opened his mouth and screamed directly into Eric's ear. The noise was excruciatingly loud, but Eric couldn't pull away. The scream filled his head, drove away all other thoughts. Scoured his mind clean.

Then, with Jimmy's barbaric cry deafening him, Eric saw shapes moving outside the windows. Large gray slithery shapes. Tentacles. They pounded up against the glass, massive rust-colored suckers pulsing in and out, fogging up the windows. Eric was terrified of those tentacles. Those suckers. And of the vague immense shape looming behind them.

Jimmy was gone, but the screaming continued. Only this time, Eric was the one screaming. And he couldn't stop. He couldn't stop screaming.

The ominous entity outside did not like Eric's screams, and its tentacles pounded the glass in fury.

Eric tried to look away, but they surrounded the room, beating against the windows, fighting to get inside. Trying to get to him. They were coming for him, and they would allow nothing to get in the way of their single-minded need to silence Eric's scream.

*H*ands held Eric down at the shoulders as he snapped awake and opened his eyes. He was back in his room in the dead of night. Hovering over him were five dark figures, black hoods lifted over their heads, faces lost in the darkness within.

"Wha—" was all he managed to say before a wet, sweet-smelling cloth was thrust over his mouth and nose. Almost instantly, his world faded to black.

*T*his time, there were no dreams.

He awoke with the bright sun baking his naked body. A slight tugging at his left arm caused his head to creak to the side, where he saw a grimy man with his back to Eric tightening a rope around Eric's wrist and tying it to a large wooden pole.

"What . . . what are you . . ."

The man straightened as if caught by surprise, then sagged. "You're awake," he said, his voice heavy with regret. "It would have been so much easier if you'd remained asleep."

The man went back to his task, tugging a bit harder on the rope now that there was no danger of waking his subject.

"What are you doing?"

"My job." He gave the rope a final tug. Then, satisfied, he stood and turned to face Eric for the first time. "Nothing personal, kid."

The man's face was heavily scarred, as if he'd been on fire or splashed with acid. He stepped over Eric's chest and grabbed his right arm, pulling it out to tie the wrist to the other end of the pole.

"Wait! Stop! Who are—"

"Quit fussing, will you? This is hard enough without you blubbering all over me. Damn, I wish the Collectors would learn to use stronger doses. It's so awkward when you're awake." He quickly strapped Eric's wrist to the pole, his movements fluid and experienced. "And so damn unfortunate."

The rest of Eric's senses kicked into gear, and he realized he was lying on a large wooden cross, to which his legs had already been bound. His eyes bulged in terror.

"You're crucifying me?"

"Well, I'm not driving any nails into your wrists, if that makes you feel any better. Just tying you up for sacrifice."

"Sacrifice? To one of those . . . those . . . monsters? They're not gods, you know. They're not gods!"

The grimy man snickered. "They're unstoppable, all-powerful, and way smarter than us. They ain't even limited to our three dimensions. We're not even ants compared to them. They can squash us with a careless thought. You tell them they ain't gods."

The man finished tying Eric to the cross, then looked at him with a frown. "You want to go upside down or right-side up?"

"What?"

"Doesn't really matter to me," he said, shrugging. "Some folks like to go upside down, like they're trying to make a statement or something. Like anybody cares. The gods don't even notice."

He stepped over Eric's head and bent down to grab the top of the cross. "But that ain't your thing, is it? Nah, didn't think so." With a grunt, the surprisingly strong man tipped the cross up, and Eric was lifted up at a slant.

Looking around, he saw he was on a dry, dusty hilltop, somewhere outside the city walls. All around him were the carcasses of dozens of wooden crosses.

"Why are you doing this?" he pleaded. "I'm just a kid! Why me?"

"Really?" the man asked as he carefully walked his hands down the length of the cross, leveraging it into a standing position. "You ain't figured it out? You doubted. Something happened—hell if I know what—and you doubted. Can't have that. All that negative energy. The gods—and I'm just gonna call them gods because why the hell not— are drawn to negativity. They can't stand it. They need to be worshipped. Loved. Somebody starts broadcasting negativity, they pick up on that. Zero in. Take care of business. You've seen what these things do when they randomly walk through a city they generally don't even know is there. Can you imagine what happens when they're actively searching for someone? Everyone dies. Whole cities cease to exist."

By now, Eric was fully vertical. There was a slight drop when the grimy man placed the foot of the cross into a hole, but Eric hardly noticed. Instead, he stared out at the clumps of blood-spattered clothing, splinters of wood, and dried chunks of past doubters that littered the ground.

"Look, not that it matters to me, but do yourself a favor and don't look at them. You're gonna die all the same; you may as well hold onto your sanity."

With that, the grimy man patted the upright cross and walked away. He headed down the hill toward some sort of rusted bunker dug out of the ground. Eric watched him yank up a heavy metal door and climb down into darkness, letting the door crash shut behind him with a deafening boom.

And Eric was alone.

He called out for help for a while but eventually gave up. The unforgiving sun marched across the sky and fell to Earth behind him, stretching his Christ-like shadow out in front of him. Just when it was maybe ten minutes from setting, when his shadow was fully twice as long as he was high, Eric caught a whiff of a familiar stench. Faint at first, it grew steadily stronger as the sun blinked out of existence for the day and the hill was bathed in moonlight. An instant panic rose in Eric's heart, but he fought it down by holding onto his determination to look his fate in the eye.

He knew now that the reason you didn't look at the gods wasn't that your eyes would melt out of your head or any such nonsense but that if people actually saw what their 'gods' looked like, they wouldn't worship them.

Well, Eric was done worshipping. He wanted to see the monsters for what they were. As the putrid odor accosted his sinuses and rumblings in the earth announced an imminent Visitation, Eric opened his eyes wide and waited for his first sight of the monsters.

Big mistake.

*"B*ut it's not fair!" complained Bonnie. "He didn't even believe in the gods yesterday! Why would they let him Ascend?"

"Well, Bonnie Baby, I sent him to his room to pray," explained Dad. "And he just prayed a whole lot, and the gods must have been impressed by how hard he was praying and how much he wanted to be good and how much he discovered that he loved them."

"But I love them way more than he did!" challenged the little girl. "How come I don't get to Ascend?"

"Nobody knows what the gods are ever thinking, honey," said Mom. "They think on such a higher level than we can ever hope to reach. Eric just had . . . whatever it was they were looking for."

She met her husband's eyes, and he nodded.

"It's because I can't get through all the Hallelujahs without stuttering, isn't it?" accused Bonnie. "Do you think if I keep practicing and practicing and being a good girl, the gods will allow me to Ascend someday?"

Mom tried to answer, but the words got stuck in her throat, so she looked at Dad for help. He cleared his throat and plastered on his best smile.

"Yes, Bonnie. I'm sure they will."

The seven-year-old's face lit up with a new determination, far too distracted to notice the single tear sliding down her father's cheek.

SACRIFICED

Kelly Lynn Colby

*P*anic and fear overwhelmed Clauda from the moment the villagers dragged her to the sacrificial altar. The thought of the dragon slithering through the crisp mountain air to claim her as tribute filled every bit of her brain with terror, blocking any sort of physical discomfort she might have otherwise felt.

Hours later, with the sun firmly hidden behind the mountain range, all Clauda could think of was how cold she was. Couldn't they have left her a blanket or something? Why did she have to be so miserable right before she was to be torn apart by a toothy beast? Maybe she could convince the dragon to roast her first. It would be nice to feel warm again before it all ended.

Clauda rotated her wrists against the coarse rope that bound her. The knot had loosened enough for some movement, but there was still no way she could have pulled her hands free. Her shoulders throbbed from the constant strain of being stretched above her head. Her toes ached from overextending to take some of the weight off her upper body. The worst part, though, was the cold. The chill started at her extremities and worked its way into her very core, until she shivered with uncontrollable need for a fire.

A breeze rolled over the bits of snow still covering the mountain valley and assaulted Clauda like a sadistic weather pattern. "No!" she yelled out to no one, because the gods surely had abandoned her. "That's it. To the afterworld with all of you."

Clauda gripped the rope as tightly as she could with her frozen hands and hauled her feet over her head. She pulled down with her arms and pushed up with her toes against the bindings. The numbness in her hands made it easier to ignore the ripping of the skin on her wrists. For a moment, she thought the thumb of her right hand would peel off like a section of orange. Clauda didn't care. Let the dragon have the souvenir for his tribute.

Blood dripped down her arm. Clauda pushed harder with her legs and allowed her upper body to sag. She cringed as slight discomfort morphed into true agony. The open wounds lubricated her hands until she was able to slide her right hand out with a scream of triumph.

Her legs fell as she dangled from one arm and tried to catch her breath. She flexed her free hand, grateful that her thumb was still attached and all her fingers worked. The blood didn't even bother her. At least it was warm.

"You can do it, Clauda. One to go." Mustering what was left of her energy, she used the rope as leverage to pull her legs back up over her head. With her right hand free, she found it much easier to wiggle her left from its binding.

"Ha! Take that, you cowards," she shouted to the empty valley. "How dare you sacrifice a girl instead of slaying the beast."

The wind stopped like someone put a cork into a flowing keg. A colossal shadow descended over Clauda. She froze with her head down. Her instincts yelled at her to run or hide, but her mind spun, unable to make a decision.

A voice thick with the smell of sulfur washed over her. "You would find me difficult to slay."

The last word echoed against the granite mountainside. Clauda's mind gave up. Her feet took over, and she ran. Jagged pieces leftover from old rockslides bit into her feet. Just as she had when the villagers restrained her, she felt no pain, only panic.

A gust of air swept Clauda's hair over her eyes, temporarily blinding her. She stumbled forward. Her arms flailed as her body careened toward the rocky ground. A warmth embraced her shoulders, accompanied by an animal smell. Two huge talons lay over her chest, on either side of her neck. At that moment, she knew she was dinner.

And she was pissed.

As hard as she could, Clauda bit down on a reddish-brown toe. The dragon swore and released her. With a leap and a skitter, she ducked behind a boulder.

The pebbles at her feet vibrated with the dragon's rumbling voice. "That was quite unnecessary. I was only preventing you from bashing your head in. I do not relish a repeat of a few centuries ago. It was a nightmare to convince the villagers to send me another girl."

A frozen fog, formed from her heavy breathing, surrounded Clauda. She stared at the barren landscape of tumbled rocks and low shrubbery. She didn't stand a chance of escape.

Then the dragon's words sank in, and Clauda's anger bubbled up again. "Wait. Did you just say that a fleeing girl bashed her head in and the problem was you had to get another sacrifice?"

"It was very inconvenient."

A flap of wings followed by a rush of air over the rock spooked Clauda into peeking over the rolled-smooth gray granite. Dragons were big. Everyone knew they were big. But this scaled burnt-amber creature was so much more than that. Clauda had seen villages that took up less land. He sat patiently on his haunches, his wings neatly folded against his back. His tail swished across pebbles and kicked up weakly rooted shrubbery.

Why didn't he do anything? The rugged talon she had so brazenly bitten could have easily picked up the boulder and tossed it aside like a rotten egg from the henhouse. Over his obtuse nose, which leaked tendrils of steam, his forward-facing ochre eyes stared at her, unblinking.

Exhaustion sank into every bone as Clauda realized she was trapped. This was it for her. "Fine. Just make it quick, okay?" With her last bit of bile, she spat, "And you should still burn Benton to the ground. That rotten town doesn't deserve to be saved by my sacrifice."

If this was to be her final moment, she wanted to die knowing her treacherous village would be next.

She leaned against the rock and waited for the teeth. It would only hurt for a second. Clauda tried to cross her arms over her chest but pulled them back as pain shot through her torn wrists. At least, she hoped it would only hurt for a second.

The dragon's head snaked down to Clauda's level. She didn't particularly want to watch her body be torn apart, but she couldn't seem to completely close her eyes. Through a gap just large enough to see the sparkle of bright-white, crazy-sharp teeth, she watched the dragon exhale warm steam that blew back her hair.

Warmth tingled on her skin, bringing it back to life. Her torn wrists itched as skin stretched over the open wounds. Clauda jerked her hands up in front of her face. The injuries were healing! The jagged tears knit together as little sparkles danced along her extremities.

Clauda twisted her hands to stretch her wrists. They still itched a bit, but she had regained total movement, and not a single scar marred her perfectly pink skin. The dragon's snout bobbed with a self-satisfied smile that only looked slightly threatening.

Anger overcame her shock, and Clauda smacked the beast's nose. "How dare you scare me like that! You could have said you were going to heal me."

Yanking his head up, the dragon loomed over Clauda. "Why would you do that? Are you deranged? I could fit your entire body in my mouth."

Before Clauda could question all her life choices, a large salty tear dropped from one of his eyes and drenched her feet. Clauda saw the dragon in a completely different light: holding her shoulder with his gentle talon, showing concern for her wounds, hovering just out of arm's reach, rubbing his nose.

She put a hand on her hip and pointed with the other. "You're not going to eat me, are you?"

With a jolt, the overly large reptile scoured the rugged landscape.

Clauda ducked as the dragon's tail swished one way and then the next, balancing the massive beast while he turned in circles.

She rubbed her bare arms, curious. "What are you looking for?"

The whites of his eyes flared as he stopped midswing to address Clauda. His hollow voice projected like that of a bad actor performing for a crowd. "It's time for us to depart so I can devour you in peace in my hidden and very secret lair."

He hopped onto the granite boulder like a large predatory bird perched on a pebble. With a swipe of his talon, he gathered Clauda in a tight grip and leaped into the air. Clauda's stomach lurched and her head throbbed with the back-and-forth motion caused by the dragon's twisting body.

Terror flooded Clauda yet again. She wrapped her arms around the toes on either side of her neck. The other two kind of curved underneath her, making a sort of seat. Clauda's head shot down as the dragon leaped into the air. Before he could fall back down, he extended mighty wings and flapped them with a deafening smack of air.

One moment, Clauda was on the ground. The next, she was higher than the daunting mountain peaks. It wasn't natural. No human being should ever be this high. She had known she'd die today. Apparently, she'd been wrong about the how.

The dragon's initial hectic movements gave way to a steady up-and-down rocking. Sitting in the dragon-talon pocket of warmth as freezing air whipped about her face, Clauda's fear morphed to wonder. Stunning mountain peaks glossed with white looked down upon a vast river of solid ice. It was almost beautiful from up here. She could smell nothing, and the wind in her ears was more comforting than complete silence.

As adrenaline dissipated, exhaustion took over. With the combination of her body being warm for the first time all day and the repetitive rhythm of the dragon's wings, Clauda lost consciousness.

A deep foreign voice floated into Clauda's cloudy mind. "Are you going to sleep all day? This will not do. You have responsibilities."

Clauda rubbed her eyes and stretched her back. A muscle along her spine screamed at the extension. After she had been hung from ropes for what felt like an eternity, her back had a bit to say about its treatment. Fully awake, Clauda jumped up as she remembered where she must be. She backed up into a headboard and surveyed her surroundings for a way out.

The dragon tapped his talons on the granite floor of an enormous cave. The walls were smooth, without a sign of tooling or natural erosion. Torches hung from the ceiling in regular intervals along each wall and in the center. No smoke rose from the light orange globes. Whatever their light source, it wasn't fire.

It wasn't at all how she had pictured the dragon's lair. Not that Clauda was a cave expert, but she had expected cramped quarters and lots of spiderwebs. Weren't there supposed to be giant spiders? All the bards described giant spiders. Admittedly, she couldn't see the floor, what with the dragon's big butt blocking the view. Maybe that was where the long-legged creepy things lived.

Sitting demurely with his tail wrapped around his haunches like a contemplative cat, the dragon coughed a bit, releasing tendrils of smoke from his nostrils. "There is no escape. I have been doing this for centuries, and I assure you, all routes have been blocked."

Why was she thinking of other huge, deadly beasts when she had the biggest and deadliest one staring at her? Then she remembered.

Clauda threw off the sheet that was covering her and stood. She stared directly into the dragon's eyes. "You said very clearly that you were going to eat me. Yet you waited for me to wake up to do the deed. You could have scarfed me down in one big swallow, and I wouldn't have known a thing about it. How cruel are you?"

The dragon blinked, then cleared his throat again. "You may call me Master, and I will call you Girl. Every morning, you will awaken at the lighting of the lamps. Then you will—"

The speech sounded rehearsed, almost routine. Clauda squinted, studying the supposedly terrifying beast. "So you're not going to eat me? Most species don't name their food before they devour it. You should make up your mind."

With a sigh, the dragon dropped his imperious head. "Look, I said what I said about eating you in the valley because I couldn't have any eavesdropping spies discover the truth. It's a lot of work to raid a village, and there are always unforeseen casualties. I've found this sacrifice-a-virgin-and-I'll-leave-you-alone plan to be much more effective."

"That's another thing. Why do you demand virgins?" Clauda smoothed down her blood-stained frock. She was mostly a virgin. Could the dragon smell the difference?

The dragon's head shot up, almost hitting the ceiling. "I don't care how you humans indulge your baser instincts. I simply don't want any children left behind without their mother."

Clauda's knees buckled as relief and confusion overwhelmed her ability to stand. She sat on the bed and crossed her legs on the rough blanket as she laid her head in her hands. "You're really not going to eat me, then."

"No. Now if you would allow me to finish my speech, you should have no more questions." The dragon once again cleared his throat, as if it were a prerequisite for speaking authoritatively.

"I'm not calling you Master." Clauda glared up at the dragon and felt like an ant defying a shoe. They never looked scared either.

"I-I—but you have to call me Master. I'm always called Master."

"And my name is Clauda, not Girl. What is your *name*?" She refused to budge, even as the steam flowing from the reddish-brown nose increased.

"Clauda? Such a ridiculous-sounding name. How am I supposed to remember that? Girl is much simpler, and I've been using it for a millennium. It's worked fine." His head curved down closer to her, though he remained out of arm's reach. "And my name is Master."

She raised a hand to push her hair out of her face. When the dragon flinched, Clauda's lip curled up on one side. He didn't want to get close enough for her to smack him again. So Clauda did have some power over this beast. "Master isn't a name. What do your dragon friends call you?"

His head shot back up, and his talons scraped the floor. "Why, I don't—they don't—what if you called me Father?"

"Nope. I already had one of those."

His back leg scratched a spot under his delicate wing. "Daddy?"

Clauda waved her arms. "Oh no, that means something, um . . . wrong to humans. Why can't I call you by your mother-given name?"

His foot dropped to the ground, and his face sagged. "No one calls me that."

"Then maybe it's time you tried. Apparently, we're going to be spending a lot of time together, since there's no escape." Clauda didn't believe there was no escape, but if she pretended she had no hope, maybe the dragon would drop his guard and she could get out of there.

The dragon's head wobbled as though his thoughts were racing around, throwing it off-balance. "Fine. My mother called me Wiggle Tail."

Clauda grabbed the end of the bed before she could fall off. "Wiggle Tail?"

He scratched the back of his head with a long talon. "I know, I know. My mother had forty-seven hatchlings to name, and she was already exhausted from the whole process by the time she got to me. I swished my tail at her, so happy to have her attention, and that was that. My given name was determined by an unthinking movement in a moment of emotion." His eyes narrowed at Clauda. "Which is why you will call me Master."

Clauda's stomach vibrated as her stress morphed into true amusement. Even though she tightened her chest to contain her glee, it was no use. "Whatever you say, Master Wiggle Tail." Laughter burst from her mouth and she rolled onto her side in the first bit of happiness she'd felt in a long time.

The skin around the dragon's nose and eyes drained of all color.

His highlighted features showed complete shock at Clauda's disrespect. "Why, I have never had this much insolence from a sacrifice."

"Then maybe you should interview possible candidates instead of letting villagers grab orphans and tie them to stakes. Kidnapping is not the best way to begin any relationship."

A deep growl rolled inside the dragon's chest. The ground vibrated with its intensity. Clauda's breath caught in her throat as she pulled her knees to her chest. Maybe she'd gone a bit too far.

Swifter than Clauda would have thought possible at his size, Wiggle Tail turned his mass and stalked away, his tail dragging dejectedly behind him. "We'll start again tomorrow morning. Maybe you'll be ready to hear my speech then." His head reached over his shoulder in such a snake-like manner that Clauda scooted back, afraid he would change his mind and snack on her anyway. "You'll get hungry eventually."

The room lightened once the dragon's massive body no longer blocked many of the lamps. Clauda pinched her nose as fetid air was whipped up by the dragon's movement. She immediately found the source of the foul odor. Before her lay the messiest living quarters she'd ever seen, and that included those of Widow Francine, who refused to throw anything away. Dark amber dragon scales were piled in the corners. Moth-eaten cloth bags littered the floors. Bits of gristle and bone, which Clauda hoped wasn't human, were scattered across the ground by a swish of the dragon's tail. Surrounding a hearth cut into the wall across from Clauda lay pots as big as wheelbarrows, caked with dried, burnt food.

With all the filth, Clauda wondered if she should worry about giant cockroaches instead of giant spiders. A commotion under the bed caught her attention as a family of rats rushed from their hiding place to a layer of rotting vegetation against the wall.

Clauda squealed and rushed after the dragon. "Wait." She had to jog to keep up, even though the dragon moved at a stately, unhurried pace. "You can't just leave me in all that filth." She swallowed hard. "There are rats."

"Yes, well, rats live in caves." Wiggle Tail looked down at Clauda as the pair passed into another room. "Now go about your business and straighten up. I have important experiments to perform."

Clauda stopped dead in her tracks and took in the full disaster that must once have been an elaborate workroom of some sort. "The gods have a sense of humor. They have to." She pulled her hair back with both hands. "You're telling me you have this elaborate ruse going with Benton just so you can get a maid?"

Wiggle Tail pushed a stack of trough-sized wooden bowls into a basin, clearing enough flat surface for him to open a large book. "If you had deigned to hear my speech like a proper servant, I would have explained all that."

"Now that is genius, Wiggle Tail. What's next?" Clauda jumped aside as the horned tail came too close for comfort.

"You polish, and I work."

Clauda crossed her arms. "And if I refuse?"

He flipped the pages of his book without glancing down. "Then you don't eat."

She was awfully hungry, but it wouldn't be the first time. This was much more important. After years of bouncing from home to home, Clauda knew the initial negotiations were crucial for setting the tone of the living arrangements. She strolled to the steps next to the basin and climbed up to the table. She wondered how many other girls had done the same.

She studied the book as if she knew what she was looking at. "What kind of work do you do?" For the first time in her life, Clauda wished she could read. She needed to understand what motivated this dragon so she could pull a con of her own and get out of this horrible place. If she wanted to cook and clean her life away, she would have married that nice boy who had proposed to her.

Wiggle Tail cocked his head at Clauda like a cat studying a fly. Seeming to reach a decision, he refocused on his book and turned another page. "I'm an alchemist."

"Huh." Clauda dug up a relatively straight splinter from the table to push through her rolled up hair. She needed it all out of her face. It was the only way she could think. "What's an alchemist?"

The dragon sighed. "I manipulate chemicals and metals in order to transmute one into another."

Clauda couldn't find any reason to change one thing into another. Unless . . .

"Can you change a blade of grass into a roasted leg of lamb?" Her stomach growled, belying her sense of control.

"Hmph. You might not want to fulfill your role, but your hunger demands satisfaction." Without looking at her directly, the dragon pointed a talon out the door to the disaster of a main room.

Clauda flung herself backward onto the table. In a huff, she flopped her arms out and stared at the dark ceiling. "Fine. I'll do some picking up."

Wiggle Tail clapped his tail against the ground. "Excellent. There is a kit in the trunk by your bed that has everything you'll need."

Forcing herself to stand, Clauda trudged down the steps to tackle what she could in the main room. She had cleaned up after the butcher for a whole year. Surely, this couldn't be worse.

The true scale of her task hit Clauda as she followed the trail the dragon's tail had snaked through the muck on the ground. The container by her bed was massive for a normal trunk but too minuscule to hold enough supplies to tackle this disaster. Why did Wiggle Tail kidnap humans? Clauda thought he might need mountain trolls to even begin finding the floor.

Still sore from their stretch on the sacrificial stake, her shoulders cursed the strain as she pushed open the large lid. The creak of rusty hinges was amplified by the size of the room as it bounced along the granite walls.

Inside the trunk was a bottle the size of a milk jug containing some sort of viscous liquid and bright white linens. There were neither brooms nor scrub brushes nor buckets. Not even a bag to shove the rotting vegetables into on their way to the compost pile. She looked behind the box. Maybe that spot crawling with rats was the compost pile. She shoved aside the cleanest linen she had ever seen to locate torches or some other means for burning everything. That would have been an improvement over the room's current condition.

Finding nothing useful, she dropped the lid in disgust. With her hands on her hips, she decided that starting somewhere was better than just standing around hungry.

A dragon scale leaned against the adjacent wall as if haphazardly tossed aside. It reminded her of the dog hair piling up in the corner of Farmer Gerock's front room. Did dragon's shed?

Clauda pushed the scale off the wall. It wobbled on the floor like an upside-down turtle, but it wasn't made of shell. She rubbed the dull inside and knocked on it. The gentle tink and cool feel of it on her knuckles suggested metal. How could something alive be covered in metal? She wondered if it were valuable.

With a strong grip on the edge, Clauda leaned back, using her mass to get the thing moving. With uncomfortably small backward steps, Clauda managed to drag the enormous scale next to the fireplace. She didn't know where else to put them, so for now she'd just pile them up.

As she rolled another scale toward her growing pile, Clauda knew she should be looking for an escape, but she was just too tired. Maybe after dinner, assuming Wiggle Tail slept, she'd have some time to snoop around.

The next scale screeched against the wall on its way to the floor. Clauda cringed at the grating sound.

Wiggle Tail peeked his head out of his laboratory. "What are you doing in there? You should be polishing, not producing unbearable sounds."

Sweat poured from Clauda as she glared at her unreasonable master. "You must be joking. How am I supposed to do any sort of polishing when I can't even find the floor? What happened to your other girl? What did she do all day?"

Wiggle Tail sighed. "I forgot you refused to allow me my speech. Everything would have been clear immediately, and we would be well on our way."

With exaggerated effort, the dragon dragged himself away from his work. "Take the cloth and polisher from your trunk and follow me."

Clauda plopped down on the floor and crossed her arms. "No."

Wiggle Tail stopped a few yards from Clauda, though his size made him seem a whole lot closer. "No? What do you mean no?"

"I've been cleaning for a while now, and I'm starving. I'm not moving until I get food."

Scratching at a spot on his shoulder, Wiggle Tail studied Clauda. "Fair."

A scale fell and clattered to the ground as he made his way to the cooking fireplace. Clauda groaned and got to her feet. "I'm going to take a nap. Let me know when it's ready."

Wiggle Tail looked like he was about to argue, but Clauda ignored his raised front talon and headed straight to her filthy sleeping blanket.

Clauda's eyes blinked open at the most gods-blessed smell she had ever experienced. She kicked her threadbare blanket aside and jumped to her feet, which she immediately regretted. After hours of dragging scales as wide as windmill wheels and as heavy as cart horses, Clauda's back screamed no matter which direction she moved. Her stomach was even more boisterous.

Half bent over like an ancient medicine woman, she limped to the warm surface by the fire. Wiggle Tail stirred an enormous cauldron with an even more impressive spoon. Clauda wondered who had made such items. Was there a dragon kitchenware vendor somewhere?

Wiggle Tail scratched his belly, and a scale dropped to the floor with a spark.

Clauda glared at the dragon. "Can't you clip or groom or whatever the heck you do for scale shedding in one spot and then gather them all into a neat pile? Dragging those scraps of metal across the floor is impossible for me. Why didn't you kidnap a troll or something much stronger?"

Her words must have hit a nerve, for Wiggle Tail itched his right flank with his back claw. Another scale clattered to the ground, soliciting a groan from Clauda.

The dragon's amber nostrils paled white in what Clauda recognized as embarrassment. As the dragon offered her a bowl that looked like little more than a thimble in his hand, he refused to meet Clauda's eyes. "Trolls are not a fitting servant for what I need you to do."

Clauda forgot to yell at the dragon as the savory smell of the warm meal distracted her. She sipped a generous amount of the salty broth. It burned her tongue, but she didn't care. She blew steam out through parted lips like a mini-dragon, but she didn't slow down.

The warmth traveled through her limbs. Through the heat, Clauda's taste buds were greeted with some of the most complex flavors she'd ever experienced. A touch of a bitter herb blended beautifully with some sort of acidic element. She moaned in ecstasy as the most tender morsel of meat almost melted in her mouth.

"By the gods, you have a talent, Master Wiggle Tail!"

Cocking his head, Wiggle Tail ladled another serving into her bowl. "My hobby has brought me much experience with mixing chemicals and textures, which is all cooking really is."

Clauda mumbled through a mouthful of food. "Forget the orchestry—"

"Alchemy."

"Alchemy. You should open a tavern. People would come from far and wide to eat this soup." Clauda pulled a calendula bud from her bowl and sucked off the faded orange petals one at a time. The bitter bite sent satisfaction through to the tips of her toes.

"Cooking is a passion of mine. I grow the herbs in my garden for other alchemical experiments." He sipped his dinner right off the spoon. "When I feel I've wasted an entire day with zero results from my experiments, I quite enjoy finding success in a well-cooked dinner."

Clauda sagged as she realized she would be expected to wash the cauldron, which could fit a cart within it. "I don't understand how your 'girls' cleaned for years at a time. I'd need a few horses just to move that cauldron."

Wiggle Tail laughed, a jaunty vibration that shook the floor just enough to knock some dust from a nearby lamp. "I do not require servants to clean the caves. They flood once a year with the spring melt. I'm satisfied with that frequency. I clean my laboratory equipment, and the pots and pans get cleaned with fire."

To demonstrate, he picked up one of the dirty bowls by the fireplace and blew a healthy dose of fire into the center. The bits of food caked on the side flared as the smell of sulfur competed with the delicious savoriness of the soup. He knocked the edge on the mantel, and the burnt bits slid out of the bowl and into the roaring fireplace. Wiggle Tail held up the clean dish with a flourish.

Clauda clapped appreciatively. "So if you have all of this under control, I'll just be on my—"

She froze as a single talon touched her chest.

"You have a much more vital role to play."

Clauda's arms dropped to her sides. "But you said . . ."

He gulped down the last of his soup and motioned for Clauda to follow him. She reluctantly jogged to catch up before his swishing tail could take out her legs.

The dragon marched through a corridor Clauda had missed earlier. She hadn't even seen the break in the wall. She put one hand on Wiggle Tail's belly to guide her way. How was she supposed to clean something she couldn't see?

Before Clauda could collapse in an outright panic over the deep darkness, a glimmer of light danced up ahead. It looked like it came from around a corner, but it was difficult for Clauda to discern around the bulk of the dragon. The light increased slowly enough that it didn't blind Clauda, though its shimmer seemed to suggest water. Oddly yellow-colored water.

Clauda crouched closer to the dragon's gut as his legs scrunched together to squeeze around a bend tight for him, though enormous for a human. The corridor opened into a room almost as big as the front one that had the same light orange lanterns hanging from the ceiling. Instead of the light getting soaked up by the grime and filth on the floor, this light shimmered and shined off the ceiling, walls, and Wiggle Tail's scales.

The dragon pushed Clauda forward with his tail. "This is your duty for as long as I allow you to stay."

She stumbled over the uneven surface until she could see the contents piled on the floor. The untarnished glitter of the precious metal spread out to fill the storage space with coins, jewelry, bars, and chalices. "Gold. By the generous love of the gods, I didn't know this much wealth was possible!"

Wiggle Tail puffed out his chest with obvious pride. "I have an impressive collection, which you are responsible for keeping spotlessly clean and neatly piled and categorized. The data for each piece in my collection has been recorded in those tomes." He gestured to a human-sized desk to the left of the entrance.

Clauda swallowed hard.

Wiggle Tail's eyes watered, and Clauda was sure he was on the verge of tears. She didn't know why he would be crying. She was the one who couldn't read.

Before Clauda could find a way to confess her inadequacy, Wiggle Tail turned his head to the side and sneezed. A disorderly pile of gold nuggets tumbled from its hill and spilled across the ground like an avalanche. The dragon skittered back into the hallway.

Clauda picked up one of the nuggets. It was heavier than it looked. Then again, how would she know what a golden nugget was supposed to feel like? She'd never seen the precious metal in real life. If she could escape with a pocketful of these, she'd be set for life.

"So I'm supposed to . . ."

Wiggle Tail pushed his body against the wall, his eyes wide and one front claw pulled back. He looked like Clauda had felt when the rats crawled out from under her bed.

She held up the gold, and the dragon recoiled his neck as far back as it would go. "Are you afraid of your treasure?"

"No, that would be silly. I'm a dragon, and dragons hoard gold. It's what we do. What's there to be afraid of?" Wiggle Tail inhaled sharply.

For a moment, Clauda thought he'd had enough of her insolence and would roast her. Then she noticed red blotches where his scales parted around his chest. "Are you okay . . . ?"

He sneezed again. This time, a wimpy flame burst over Clauda's head, forcing her to drop to the ground. The dragon turned his bulk in the tight corner and hurried down the corridor.

"Wait!" Clauda cried. "What just happened?"

By the time she made her way through the dark hallway, Wiggle Tail was stirring the cauldron of soup violently. Clauda stayed a bit back to avoid the splashes of scalding hot liquid. The dragon pointedly ignored her.

Instead of fear, though, Clauda felt empathy. She'd seen this reaction before when she worked for Widow Francine. "You're allergic to gold, aren't you?"

He dropped the spoon and scratched his belly with both front talons. "I've been trying to produce a hypoallergenic gold variety with my alchemical experiments, but with little success."

"Little success?"

"Well, I can produce gold, but every scrap still gives me these horrible hives and makes me sneeze."

Clauda's mind spun with the possibilities. "Are you saying you can make gold in that filthy lab of yours?"

"Well, gold, yes, certainly. That's what the pile of nuggets is from. That's one of your jobs. To transport the gold from the lab to the storage facility, as far away from me as possible." Wiggle Tail wiped a tear from his eye.

An idea formed in Clauda's mind. If it worked, being sacrificed to a dragon might have been the best thing to ever happen to her. "I remember seeing calendula in the soup. Do you happen to have coriander and perchance some oil to blend it all together?"

With a shake of his head, Wiggle Tail slunk toward his laboratory. "If all you can think about is your belly, then our conversation is through. I have work to do, and so do you." He mumbled something about talking too much to a simple-minded human.

"No, no, no. It's not to eat. I can make you an ointment to soothe your itchy rash." Clauda's words froze Wiggle Tail in his tracks. "I can't cure the condition, but I can make living with the gold much more bearable."

His head snaked over his folded wings to stare down at her. "You can make the itching stop?"

Clauda straightened her back and clasped her hands. "I'm confident I can. It was one of the most common salves I made for Widow Francine."

"Then follow me."

*G*ently lifting a belly scale, Clauda smoothed on the last bit of freshly mixed salve. "That's the last of it. You'll have to grow more coriander before I can make another batch."

"I haven't felt this comfortable for, well, for centuries." Wiggle Tail earned his name as his long appendage whipped back and forth across the floor like a wagging dog's.

"I'm glad I could help." After washing her hands, Clauda took in the incredible greenery of the cave garden. "How do you get these plants to grow without the sun?"

"I don't."

Clauda pressed herself against a wall as the dragon stretched up to the ceiling, his tail balanced his body as he stood on his back legs. He blew a steady stream of fire against the roof above until it glowed a soft brown-orange, like his scales. Water dripped from cracks like rain. Unbothered by the heat of the rock, Wiggle Tail slid the ceiling back, exposing the open blue sky above.

The sunlight seemed impossibly bright to Clauda, even though she'd only been in the cave for a day or so. Freezing water poured down into an irrigation system set up to catch the spillage and filter it down to the thirsty plants below.

"Incredible." Clauda gawked at the ingenuity as the dragon landed back on all fours. "You could have been burning down villages and sitting on your captured hoard, but instead you've invented a way to grow food in the middle of winter."

After adjusting a leaking pipe, Wiggle Tail moved around the room, making sure the plants received the light and water they needed.

"Well, I couldn't very well sit on my hoard, now could I? I will never be a proper dragon. It's so embarrassing to be allergic to the one thing that defines who you are."

"Why does it have to define who you are?" Clauda put her hands on her hips. "People have been trying to tell me who I am my whole life. Curse them, I say. I am whoever I choose to be." She pointed at the dragon. "You can be whoever you choose to be."

Scratching his head, Wiggle Tail seemed to consider Clauda's words. "I love growing my plants and experimenting with alchemy."

"What's holding you back?"

"Supplies, servants." He coughed to the side. "Shame."

"Seriously?" Clauda jumped onto the edge of the planter nearest Wiggle Tail and motioned him down to her. "Now pay attention because I think you need to hear this."

His warm breath enveloped Clauda three times before she was sure she had his full attention. "You are a DRAGON!" she yelled.

His head retreated, but only a couple of inches.

"You can do whatever you want." She motioned to the marvel of technology around her. "Do you know how much the villagers—curse the gods, the whole kingdom—would give to be able to grow food in the winter? You've figured it out. With that hoard of gold of yours that makes you so miserable, you could buy up land and pay—yes, I said pay—workers to be your hands on the ground."

Wiggle Tail's eyes roamed the ceiling and the planters. "Hmmm . . ."

"Hmmm, what? You've tricked villagers into giving you servants forever. Why not just hire a bunch and end the stupid ruse?"

"That would certainly allow me more time to work on my experiments. I bet I could improve this marvelous lotion you've made for me. I know I'm not the only dragon who has allergies."

Clauda thought of a final touch. "Plus, it would give you a whole audience to feed. That cauldron would satisfy the village for a week, and they would be happy for it."

"I do find delight in others enjoying my recipes." Wiggle Tail eyed

Clauda like he just thought of something. "I suppose you wish to be released when these others take your place?"

Clauda crossed her arms. "No, I like it here. Besides, who would make the balm for you until you discover a hypertonic—"

"Hypoallergenic."

"Hypoallergenic gold." Clauda paced along the planter's edge. "I could manage your human workers and make sure they get a fair wage without your delicate, little talons having to touch the gold."

Before he could change his mind, Clauda thrust her hand out. "Deal?"

Wiggle Tail looked confused until Clauda shook her hand up and down and pointed to his. Placing the tip of one talon in her hand, he allowed her to move it up and down.

"Now you say, 'deal.'"

"Deal."

Satisfied, Clauda jumped down from the planter. "I do have one request before we get started."

Rubbing his eyes, the dragon shook his head. "Aren't the caveats supposed to come before the deal is struck?"

Clauda shrugged. "This is important."

"I'm sure it is."

Her face drained of color as she thought about her neighbors and how they had callously left her to be devoured by a dragon, how they'd been doing the same thing to other girls for centuries. "Benton doesn't get in on this. Not a single resident of that gods-cursed place gets to see a speck of your gold."

Wiggle Tail's face lengthened as he seemed to grow as serious as Clauda. "Agreed."

Wiping her face to change her mood, Clauda marched through the door. "Also . . ."

With a great sigh, Wiggle Tail trailed after her. "There's more?"

Clauda stopped at the entrance to the muck-coated, foul-smelling main cave. "This place gets a good scrubbing before any other work gets done."

Wiggle Tail's deep laugh filled the chamber with joy. "As you command, Master Clauda."

Standing with her legs parted and her hands on her hips, Clauda liked the sound of that. "We're going to make a great team, Master Wiggle Tail."

RUBANS MAGNIFIQUES

Rebekah Aman

"The splash of dark crimson across the monochromatic checkered background truly captures the imagination. It is a simple image, but there are endless meanings behind it." The balding head with tuffs of gray hair over each ear nodded with a content smile. "My girl, you have joined the exhibit. Congratulations!"

For a moment, Sophie couldn't believe what she was hearing. She stood motionless, replaying the last two statements in her mind. Then, slowly, a grin crept across her face.

"Really?" she asked softly. *Please don't let this be my imagination.*

"Really, my girl." The gallery owner turned to smile at her. "Well done."

A small yip of excitement escaped before Sophie managed to reign in her emotions to appear slightly more professional. "Thank you! Thank you so much for this opportunity, Mr. Nahum. I cannot tell you what it means to me that you are willing to display my piece here in your gallery."

"Perseverance pays off in the end, my girl. Don't forget that. Now, come back tomorrow afternoon at three, and we will attend to the onerous business side, but tonight, you celebrate your achievement.

Not everyone gets a chance to display their work in my gallery, after all."

"Yes, of course, thank you. Thank you!" Sophie practically skipped from the building.

Finally, after nearly two years of failure, she had managed to get her artwork in a museum. And not just any museum, but Mr. Nahum's art gallery, Magnifique. Sophie released a full-force squeal, startling a passerby on the sidewalk. If this went well, and if she continued getting inspiration for new and beautiful pieces, she could finally live her dream of becoming an artist instead of taking odd jobs here and there.

She had done a little bit of everything. The typical waitress and cashier jobs had been her first stints, but she'd grown bored with them. There wasn't enough color to inspire her. Then she'd had a job as an administrative assistant, and that had been truly awful. She had felt the creativity leaching from her pores as the hours ticked by. For a year and a half, she had done a rapid series of random jobs: photographing for a small newspaper, mowing lawns, spinning signs, acting as a guinea pig for psychological and lab experiments, selling cell phones, then vacuum cleaners, then comic books, weaving baskets and making necklaces for a small seaside shop—that one had actually been enjoyable, but money had been too tight for them to keep on an extra employee.

Truthfully, Safe Harbor offered a wide range of vocational opportunities. It was somewhat remote, but it was always crawling with tourists. The seascapes of the north Atlantic were gorgeous, and the town was wrapped snuggly in a blanket of trees that provided a lovely venue for hiking in the summer. Sophie had grown up here; she adored it. There was artistic inspiration in every direction, but the typical vistas were the subjects of most art pieces.

It wasn't until six months ago, when she found a very peculiar job that required intense cleaning, that she realized she could not move ahead as an artist until she found her own unique subject and style. She could not continue painting what everyone else painted and expect to get ahead. With that epiphany, she had realized that her newest employer provided her with an intriguing subject.

There she had sat, for her very first assignment, on the edge of a large parlor with a black-and-white marble-tiled floor. A staircase roamed upward in a leisurely curve to her left. Large, intricately carved wooden doors stood proudly at her back. Before her was the purpose for her employment. There was a broken table off to one side that must have held the lovely vase of flowers that was by then scattered all around in sharp bits and leafy pieces. However, that part of the cleaning had not been the reason for her signature on a nondisclosure agreement. It was the remainder of the rather impressive mess that had necessitated the extra layer of security.

Her conscience had screamed at first—murders were supposed to be reported!—but then she had remembered the large sum of money that had appeared on the bedside table, the nicely furnished room that had been supplied to her in this impressive home, and the fantastic meals supplied by a personal cook, and her conscience had quieted a bit. At least there hadn't been a body for her to dispose of, but the amount of blood splattered about would take hours to remove, even with the extremely heavy-duty cleaning implements that had been provided.

Her eyes had roamed over the scene, and as they passed over it yet again, she had found herself admiring the gruesome beauty of it. Chaos reigned in this world. Society tried to tame it with walls, schedules, and vases of flowers, but in the end, walls crumbled, schedules unraveled, vases broke, and all that was left of the human life was a puddle of glistening blood on the floor. It was odd that she could smile amid the horror and gore, but she had smiled. She had also thanked her lucky stars that she had been the one chosen for this job.

As quickly as she could, she had made that foyer spotless. Then she'd run upstairs to her room and begun painting. That very painting was the one accepted today at Magnifique.

Now, as she left the art gallery, the thought that there was most likely something wrong with her crossed her mind. She may very well be arrested in the future for failing to report a crime and for cleaning up the evidence. However, she had finally made her mark on the artistic world.

August air mingled well with sugary confections and rich cocoa, so Sophie popped into her favorite bakery and ordered a scone and hot chocolate to go. Sustenance in hand, she wandered over to a nearby park and plopped down on a bench. Some children played on a swing set, runners swept past on the wide sidewalk, a yoga class was being held in the grass up ahead, and a father and daughter were flying a pink kite.

Sophie felt her conscience twinge a bit, but that had been happening less frequently. She hadn't ever met her employer, even though it seemed they lived in the same house. There was a rigid man who always wore a suit named Mr. Trent, who seemed to be her employer's businessman. Mr. Trent had been the one who brought the nondisclosure agreement and employee forms. He had also been the one who informed her of the location of the cleanups, and Sophie assumed he was the one who had left the cash on her bedside table as well. With a slight shiver, she made a mental note to install a second lock on her door and talk to him about an alternate location for dropping off her wages.

As Sophie popped the last bite of scone into her mouth, she found herself wondering about her employer. Who could it be? Someone with violent tendencies, obviously, and someone with quite a bit of money. Over the last several months, Sophie had also wondered who the victims might have been. She would hear of a missing person on television and think that perhaps she had just finished cleaning them up. In fact, she was memorializing them on canvas . . . or their blood, anyway.

It was easier not knowing who the victims were, but she was growing more and more curious about her employer. She felt a strong sense of gratitude toward the man or woman who had given her such glorious subject matter. She would have liked to thank him or her.

Sophie began to feel light-headed, and she shook her head slightly. *Not again . . .*

*H*er pocket was vibrating. Sophie gradually swam toward consciousness and blinked her eyes open. It was dusk, which meant she had been asleep for a few hours.

"Really?" Sophie grumbled as she pushed herself up from where she had slumped down on the bench. She saw that her empty cup of cocoa had fallen to the ground. "This has to be more than low blood sugar. I need a new doctor."

Her phone buzzed in her pocket again. Mr. Trent had texted her about a job. Fortunately, it was at the house.

Sophie stood and tossed her empty cup into a trash can before making her way back home. The cleanup was in the parlor this time, and Sophie stood in the doorway, surveying the mess. She hated it when the jobs occurred in carpeted areas of the house. With a sigh, she pulled on her gloves and mask and sprayed the super-heavy-duty cleaning solution over the red-splattered white couch, the blood-soaked chartreuse carpet, and the spattered yellow curtains.

This job was more contained than the one that had occurred in the upstairs master bedroom last week, and the coffee table, though in disarray, was surprisingly intact. When the dining room had been the murder scene, the solid-oak table had been splintered into several pieces. Sophie straightened up the table while she waited for the cleaning solution to do its work, but her tidying didn't take long. She leaned back against the wall.

She had cleaned up nearly every room in this house at one point or another; some of them more than once. Her curiosity prompted her to snoop around in each room, but she had never found any clues about her employer. She had been certain that the master bedroom would be a treasure trove of information, but the closet and bathroom had been locked, and the rest of the room appeared to be un-lived-in.

Not every job had been inside, though. She also received odd jobs that cropped up outside the house, and those required expedited service. They were always in the middle of the night, but each had provided another image she could capture on canvas, so she was happy to put up with the inconvenience.

Wind brushed across her cheek, and Sophie realized that the bottom pane of the window had been broken. The breeze ruffled the curtains, and the glass on the floor reflected the red and yellow beautifully. She sat mesmerized for a moment before bursting into action to finish cleaning. She had to get to her paints to capture the image. As twisted as her employer must be, somehow every scene created had beauty to it. She would love to have a conversation about that and show her employer how she memorialized what would otherwise be so fleeting an image.

Sophie decided she would ask Mr. Trent if she could meet her employer. He had begun eating dinner with her on occasion, and tonight was lasagna night—the cook at the massive house was very gifted. Mr. Trent would definitely make an appearance. Yes, one way or another, Sophie was going to uncover the identity of her mystery employer.

"*S*o, Mr. Trent," Sophie mumbled around a mouthful of fluffy handmade bread that had been created as a side to the delicious main dish. "How long have you worked for my *mysterious* employer?"

Mr. Trent delicately dabbed at his mouth with his napkin before folding and resettling the linen back on his lap. He sucked in a deep breath and slowly turned his head toward Sophie.

"I believe you were told at the time you were hired to limit all questions to your job and especially your employer. Am I mistaken?" One perfect eyebrow slowly rose to punctuate his query. It was clear that he was well aware he was not mistaken, but just as a parent would with a child, he wished for Sophie to recall and accept that edict on her own.

Sophie's lips tightened, and she glowered at him. "I've been working here for about six months. Have I done anything to make you think that I am untrustworthy? Is my work unsatisfactory?"

"If either were the case, you would no longer be employed," Mr. Trent stated curtly before taking a bite of lasagna.

"Then I think I deserve a reward, and the reward that I want is a teensy bit of information. I'm not going to tell anyone. Besides, I'm asking about *you* and how long *you* have been employed. I'm not asking about my employer."

A full minute ticked by as Mr. Trent contemplated and chewed. Finally, he set his fork down, took a sip of water, dabbed at his lips with the napkin, and carefully replaced it again.

"I do not work for your employer."

"Huh?" Sophie grunted.

"I do not work for your employer," Mr. Trent repeated.

"I heard you the first time, but . . ." Sophie shook her head. "What is that supposed to mean? You do everything my employer wants. You handle the paperwork and the payments and the assignments. Who do you work for, then?"

"My organization and your employer have a mutually beneficial arrangement that could be terminated at any time, though I do not expect that to occur." A small smile played at the corner of Mr. Trent's lips.

Sophie plopped an elbow on the table and squashed her cheek into her palm, her saucy fork just barely angled away from her face. "So what's your organization?"

"Because my organization is so very closely tied to your employer, whom you are aware we are not to discuss, I do not feel I should disclose any additional information on this matter."

Sophie scrunched her nose. "But doing the bidding of my employer can't be the only thing your organization does."

"It isn't."

"What else do they do, then?"

Mr. Trent gave her a secretive half smile. "If I told you that, you would begin to understand a little more about your employer."

Sophie heaved a great sigh and took a bite of lasagna. She was clearly going to get no further with this line of questioning. She was just going to have to figure this out for herself.

They finished their dinner in silence, and Sophie trailed Mr. Trent to the door as he took his leave. She wasn't entirely certain why she was following him, except maybe in the vain hope that he would take pity on her and give her a few more crumbs of information. He remained silent as he opened one of the grand doors and stepped onto the stoop. Then he paused.

"Curiosity can be a dangerous thing, Sophie. Oftentimes, after we've discovered the object of our interest, we find ourselves wishing we had never learned the secret." He spoke softly as he stared out into the night. Then he locked sad eyes with hers. "This is one of those secrets, Sophie. We are simply protecting you."

With that, he shut the door, and Sophie stood in the empty foyer alone. A grandfather clock chimed loudly from the sitting room down the hall.

Her brows drew together in thought as she whispered aloud. "If my employer is so dangerous, then why am I staying in his home?"

She had never really thought about it before. She knew that her employer killed people, but she had always just assumed she would be safe since she was needed for cleanup. However, if she needed protection, maybe she wasn't quite as safe as she had thought.

Sophie climbed the stairs to do a little painting before bed. Somehow, she still wasn't scared, just more curious. Instead of turning toward the empty canvas propped up on an easel, she moved over to the old, scarred desk in her room—most certainly an expensive antique—and pulled out a pen and some paper. She also opened her laptop and began searching on the browser.

Well into the night, she made lists and took notes of all the times she had cleaned, where it had been, and what she had seen around the site, and she compared them to the news reports she found for the local area. There had to be a pattern, and if she could find the pattern, then she could find her employer.

Sophie liked to think that people were given a set number of attributes at birth, which she pictured as a bundle of colorful ribbons. Some babies were given lots of intelligence ribbons, some had more representing athletic talent or agility, and several would be given varying abilities with no one attribute excelling over the others. Over time, if a skill wasn't practiced, it would be like the wind had captured the ribbon and carried it off to a distant land.

As for herself, Sophie had a handful of creative and artistic strips of cloth, and she had been holding onto those tightly to ensure the wind could not take one away. Because she was so very gifted in that one area, there wasn't room in her hand for many other attributes. That had never bothered her much before. Now that she was attempting to uncover a secret, though, she truly wished she had been given a few ribbons of intelligence to brighten up her bundle.

She could pull up articles on killings in the area easily enough, but since she had never seen the victims that she cleaned up, she hadn't recognized anyone. She even tried to cross-reference the cleaning locations with murder sites, but she just wasn't turning up much. She spent hours searching and gained a newfound respect for investigators. This was hard.

Finally, inspiration hit. She realized that instead of looking for murders, she should just look up Mr. Trent. She could figure out where he worked, and she was certain that would lead to her employer. Unfortunately, she did not know Mr. Trent's first name, and there were more than a few Trents in this town.

Sophie heaved a huge sigh. This was going to take more time than she had thought.

For the last month, Sophie had either tried to follow Mr. Trent or, when that inevitably failed, started making rounds to locations where men with the last name Trent worked. She had crossed off Alberts and Christophers and Jasons and Lukes and

Matthews. It was taking longer than she'd expected because she had gotten several more cleaning jobs and her piece at the art gallery had been such a huge hit that Mr. Nahum had commissioned three more. That had been the most exciting thing to ever happen, and she had smiled for days.

Now, she frowned down at the paper in her hand as she stood on the empty sidewalk before a large familiar building at just after ten in the morning. Sophie gazed back up at the building. The elaborate letters GSAW, the company's name, hung just above the door. She had come here for nearly two weeks to earn money before she moved on to another job. She didn't remember a Mr. Trent, and she certainly hadn't seen her Mr. Trent while she was there.

"Sophie!"

Her head whirled toward the sound, only to see the agitated and confident strides of Mr. Trent as he advanced on her from a short ways down the sidewalk.

Sophie gave a little wave. "Hey, Mr. Trent."

Mr. Trent stopped a little too close to her. "What are you doing here?"

"Umm . . ." Sophie's eyes wandered away from him for a moment before looking to the cracked cement, where a single yellow flower grew. It was quite pretty. "I was going to earn a little more money here."

A quick glance at Mr. Trent's face revealed that he did not believe her.

"You are paid handsomely for your current occupation, not to mention the extra you have received from the art gallery," Mr. Trent stated. "I repeat. What are you doing here?"

Sophie heaved a huge sigh. "Fine. I was looking for you."

His brows angled down sharply. "Me? And why were you looking here?"

"Because a Mr. Nicholas Trent works here." Sophie punctuated the statement by waving her list in front of him.

He took the sheet from her. "You've certainly been busy. This had to have taken some time—more time than a day and a half would afford. You saw me the day before last. So tell me, why search for a person that you see every few days?"

Sophie clasped her hands, and her cheeks warmed. "I don't know much about you, Mr. Trent. I was just trying to find out a little."

Mr. Trent was quiet as he studied her. "This behavior is quite similar to a stalker's, you realize?"

Sophie's eyes widened. "It's nothing like that, Mr. Trent! I swear!"

"Good." Mr. Trent balled up her paper and tossed it in a nearby trash can.

"Why did you do that?" Sophie exclaimed in dismay.

"To ensure that you do not continue this attempt to invade my privacy." His icy gaze pierced her. "You will cease this investigation, correct?"

Sophie hesitated a moment before nodding.

Instantly, Mr. Trent relaxed, a small smile on his face. "It's settled, then. I will escort you back to the house."

"You don't have to." Sophie shook her head. "It's not that far of a walk. The fresh air will do me good."

Mr. Trent turned on his heel and began walking. Sophie hurried to catch up. They walked in silence for a good ten minutes before Mr. Trent finally spoke.

"Why not simply investigate connections between missing persons?" he muttered softly, his brow furrowed.

"What?" Sophie asked.

Mr. Trent's eyes widened slightly as he seemed to remember he had a companion on his walk.

"Ignore me," he replied, waving his hand.

"Missing persons?" Sophie frowned as she repeated his words. "They were all murdered. They aren't missing persons; they're murder victims."

Mr. Trent chuckled. "The police do not know they—"

He cleared his throat, his face masking all emotion. "You are quite right, Sophie."

"Oh," Sophie whispered softly. She felt like a complete idiot.

Another few seconds of silence went by, during which Sophie lamented her lack of intelligence ribbons.

"Don't fret, Sophie," Mr. Trent said awkwardly. "No need to trouble yourself with all this."

"I'm dumb," Sophie said.

"Quite the opposite. Your intelligence just has a tendency to hibernate until it comes out in bursts of color."

"Really?" Sophie grinned. "That's the nicest thing you've ever said to me, Mr. Trent."

He gave a slight shrug. That was when Sophie felt a surge of inspiration.

"Say, Mr. Trent?" Sophie began.

"Hmm?"

"We've known each other for quite a while now, and you always call me Sophie, but all I can call you is Mr. Trent. Can I just drop the 'Mister' and call you Trent?"

"Nick."

"Huh?"

"You can call me Nick."

They were relatively quiet throughout the remainder of their trek to the large house. Nick dropped her off without ceremony, stated he would be joining her for dinner this evening, and then turned on his heel to make his way back to work. Sophie saw that he was following the very same course they had taken to get to the house from where she now believed he worked. She rushed upstairs to her computer and began searching—a much more limited search this time—and it did not take long before she came across an interesting blog about his workplace.

Something is going on at GSAW, and they are keeping it hidden. I've overheard hushed conversations, seen some very odd papers while filing. Asking doesn't seem to get me anywhere, but they are doing more than what it seems on the surface. I think they're testing something . . . something big.

Sophie thought this was what many people would have labeled a conspiracy blog, but it certainly caught her attention. She decided to message the writer and was surprised when she received an almost instantaneous response to her question.

I work there, so I've seen a lot of things. There are rooms that are kept locked, and I've heard them talking about this "benefactor" and his special projects.

Sophie thought a moment before she wrote back. *I've only been to GSAW a few times to earn a bit of extra cash, but now I work for a mysterious "benefactor" who has me cleaning up some pretty sensitive stuff. I believe the two might be connected.*

Really? I knew something shady was going on here. They don't think secretaries know much, but we listen and see everything. Can we talk over lunch today? Meet me at Crazy for Cocoa in an hour.

I'll be there, Sophie replied.

The woman sitting across from Sophie was attractive, but she had a level of paranoia that was a bit unsettling. She had gone on and on about weird experiments and people going missing and executives holding secret meetings. Sophie was beginning to believe she had made a terrible decision in coming here.

"I appreciate you meeting with me, Eleanor," Sophie said with a smile. "Everything you're saying sounds . . . rather sinister, though. I'm not sure I want to get mixed up in—"

Eleanor grabbed Sophie's hand, her eyes almost wild. "No! I can't do this on my own anymore. I feel like I'm always being watched."

"I'm not sure what I can . . ."

"We can search for proof!" Eleanor exclaimed. "I was going to ask you to meet me tonight at GSAW. Here."

Eleanor dug into her pocket and pushed a slip of paper into Sophie's hand.

"What is this?" Sophie asked.

Eleanor glanced around before leaning close and whispering, "Keep it safe. It's the code to get into the locked file room in the basement. I just know they'll have proof there. Meet me at nine tonight. We'll search together."

Sophie frowned as she stared at the paper in her hand. "I don't think—"

"You have to! I won't accept no for an answer." Eleanor stood. "Nine tonight."

Before Sophie could respond, Eleanor left the café. Sophie stared at the door.

"So weird," she muttered. "I think I'll pass on her nighttime investigation."

She yawned, feeling the all-to-familiar haziness encompass her.

"Oh no," she groaned, and then everything went black.

S ophie's brain was hazy and groggy as she pulled herself upward from the land of dreams. She felt like she had only been asleep for ten minutes, but she knew it had to have been longer than that. What had woken her? A cheerful melody sounded again, and she realized her phone was ringing.

"Hello?"

"Got a cleaning job for you." Mr. Trent's tones were clipped.

"Really? What time is it?"

"4:15 p.m."

"Four fifteen?" Sophie jumped out of bed—wait . . . how was she in her bedroom?

"Sophie?" Mr. Trent asked after the silence lengthened.

"Oh . . ." Sophie shook her head. "So where is the job, Mr. Trent . . . uh, Nick?"

"You know the park near the house?"

"Uh-huh." Sophie started pulling on her shoes.

"There's a café called Crazy for Cocoa."

Sophie's stomach dropped.

"Behind that building. This is an emergency job, so you must get there as quickly as possible."

"Right . . ."

Sophie ended the call and stared at her phone. Was it just a coincidence?

Please tell me you're still alive, she prayed. The woman might have been incredibly intense and strange, but Sophie didn't want anything bad to happen to her. Maybe Eleanor's paranoia wasn't completely unfounded, after all.

As usual, there was no victim or identifying information in the space Sophie was to clean. She did admire the spatter pattern against the time-worn brick and took a mental picture for her future artwork, but her mind was a whirl of emotions.

The cleanup was not nearly as messy this time—almost as if her benefactor had been less violent, as if his or her heart just wasn't in it. After an hour, Sophie scrubbed the last spot from an awkward position half-behind trash cans in the back alley. That was how she managed to find the small scrap of paper. Sophie's eyes widened, and her heart beat wildly as she recognized the small slip with the file room code. How had it ended up here? Eleanor had given it to her at the café, so it shouldn't be here.

She snatched up the paper and marched to GSAW. She remembered that they held some sleep studies, so the door should be unlocked even if most workers had gone home by now. She was able to get in without any trouble, and she walked straight to the elevator. Eleanor had said the locked file room was in the basement. Sophie pushed the B button and felt the elevator shudder into action.

Her anxiety rose as the elevator descended. The doors whisked open to reveal a brightly lit hallway, all white, with a tile floor. Sophie sucked in a deep breath and began her search. It did not take long to find the one door with a keypad to one side, and she typed in the code. A green light signaled her ability to enter.

The walls of the small room were lined with filing cabinets. Sophie grimaced before starting with the first cabinet on the left. After rifling through several files throughout the drawer, she realized that each one was marked "Failure." Scanning the labels on each drawer, Sophie saw that the cabinets on the left wall were alphabetized, and she realized they must all be failed projects. She did some spot-checking to verify her theory before moving on.

She wasn't looking for failed experiments; she needed information on her benefactor. She turned to the cabinets on the right. These were also alphabetized. Sophie found herself intrigued by the file contents. Some of the same tests that she had undergone had been performed on others. That part wasn't surprising, but the side-effects . . .

Sophie shuddered as she continued pulling files and reading them. They did not consider any of these people failures, but neither did they see them as successes. Sophie realized she wouldn't find her benefactor here either, so she turned to the back wall. Because the room was narrow, there was only one, solitary filing cabinet with two drawers. She pulled open the top drawer and found that these were not alphabetical. Instead, they had separators that indicated how successful each test had been. The front was the least successful, and she grabbed a file from there.

Subject: Henry Able

Test: Injection of mood-controlling serum #64

Result: Subject was exposed to extreme stimuli to promote fury. Serum was activated after an hour of exposure. Subject became serene within a minute. Additional exposure to stimuli did not induce any level of anger. Serum remained in effect for three hours.

"Huh," Sophie muttered before jumping to the next success level and pulling out a file.

Subject: Jenna Green

Test: Injection of enhanced-strength serum #256

Result: Subject was able to lift four times her weight without undo damage to her musculoskeletal system. Serum's effective time limit has not been determined.

Additional Notes: A week after injection, subject still shows no sign of the serum wearing off.

A month after injection, there is no change in serum's effectiveness. Three months, no change. Six months, no change. One year, no change. We believe the serum has permanently altered the subject.

Sophie's eyes widened. "Whoa. This is insane."

She closed the top drawer and pulled open the bottom one. She was about to grab a file from the next level when the very back separator caught her eye. It indicated that they had nearly reached the ultimate goal, and there was only one file in that section. Sophie pulled it out and was about to open it when her phone buzzed. It was Nick, letting her know he would be at the house in ten minutes for dinner. She had to leave!

She hugged the file to her chest as she raced to the elevator. She had to get home before he did. And after dinner, Mr. Trent would be explaining some things.

*D*inner had been excruciating, and Nick was just about ready to take his leave when Sophie finally worked up the courage to confront him. She slammed the file down on the table. With a frown, Nick glanced at it and sighed. There was no surprise on his face, just resignation.

"Explain." Sophie's eyes were hard.

"You are certain you wish to continue on this course?" Nick asked softly.

"Yes."

With a sigh, Nick turned to face her squarely and began in a soft, calm tone. "A few years back, GSAW received a large sum of money. These funds were to be used for research that was ultimately to be used to enhance our generous benefactor. He was interested in prolonging life, dampening and elevating moods, and boosting physical and mental abilities, and a bit was for discovering cures for various ailments. We began our research with little success at first, and we advertised for test subjects under innocuous terms. In fact, you applied about six months back for twenty-five hundred dollars, I believe. You were to undergo some psychological and drug testing. You were told that you were being given a shot of adrenaline, and you ran on a treadmill for thirty minutes, correct?"

Sophie nodded.

"Some of these tests resulted in the demise of the test subject, which was fairly easy to cover up. None of the experiments are legal, and our benefactor does not wish for anyone to learn of his involvement, so we ensure that all remains well hidden. But then there was one special subject. Everything seemed to work quite marvelously. She was much more brilliant, genius-level; her strength was phenomenal. Her moods . . . well, it was best to keep her happy.

"Unfortunately, her enhanced brainpower came back to haunt us. She knew the damage that would result if our secrets came to light and used that as blackmail. She is now free to do as her moods dictate, and we are forced to cover up her misdeeds to ensure that our own remain in the shadows."

"So . . . this subject . . . she's my employer?" Sophie asked.

"She is." Nick paused. "But she's more than that."

"What do you mean?"

Nick scooted the file toward her and flipped open the cover. "She's you."

"What!" Sophie found herself staring down at a small photograph of herself paperclipped to the inside cover.

"Not you, per se, but your alter ego."

"She's . . . me?"

"Yes and no, dear Sophie. You are two very distinct personalities, reminiscent of the classic novel by Robert Louis Stevenson. She likes to call herself Mistress Hyde."

SPOTLESS

A.F. Hartsell

Taking in a measured breath, I counted to ten with the exhale. Not my brightest idea, all things considered, as the room contained an artistic spray of exploded elves.

Several orcs in blue jumpsuits lumbered about cleaning up what was left of Julia and three or four of her friends. The word *Scrubber* was splashed across the back of their jumpsuits.

Trillby, the fairy in charge of cleanup for the city, was currently dashing around like a jacked-up spaniel, her shrill voice causing a nerve to twitch under my eye.

"Trill," I said calmly, trying to squash the budding headache building between my eyes by pinching the bridge of my nose.

The snobbish thing stared at me for a beat before snapping "What, *Kassandra?*" as if leaving off my formal title would upset me. I mean, it did, but I wasn't going to let her in on that.

The caste system had been legally written out of existence some seventy-five years ago, but for creatures that lived four times that long, prejudice was going to take a while to die out.

"When Caesar finds out that Julia is—"

"Mince?" I offered unhelpfully.

Trillby compressed her lips into a thin line. "He will not be pleased someone under his protection was attacked."

A tightening of her jaw let me know that Trillby was about done with me for the day.

Breaking the news to Caesar was going to be a complicated dance. The prime minister was elven, conceited, and powerful—a real blast at parties. He was going to demand answers, and right now, I didn't have any. I wasn't even sure if all of Julia was still in that room. The elven woman had been one of the prime minister's favorite consorts.

I rarely got calls for cleanups, but the occasional governmental death required my oversight. It wasn't something I had been expecting to do in my line of work, but here I was.

Mostly, I was needed to smooth over political gaffes, stave off the occasional tribal war, or keep our feuds from spilling over into the human world. We caused enough issues for ourselves without having to worry about humans getting gored while trying to take selfies with unicorns.

The fae didn't have police like the human world did. We were less apt to singularly murder one another, as most clashes were during wartime.

We had a sanitation crew to keep us off the radar, but not a real investigative body. Fae didn't really care about human kills, and the rare time there was a fae-on-fae murder, it was normally straightforward and dealt with by whoever took a revenge oath—usually a family member.

"I will handle it," I soothed, hoping the pale creature would pass out from lack of oxygen before I gave into the urge to swat her across the room. "Treat this as any other cleanup."

Trill spun around, her blue eyes scrunching together in annoyance. "We've never had to scrub a dignitary's consort, Kass! My gods, the prime minister. My career is over."

If only.

I sighed and shrugged my too-wide shoulders. "Not our job to keep them safe," I intoned pragmatically. "That's on Warden and the Sentinels. Purify the room and leave the politics to me."

Trillby cast me a scornful glance before flitting off with a terse nod. Good thing I was an empath. How else could I guess what the little thing was thinking?

Aiming to leave the well-appointed condo, I nodded to one of the orcs, who was a good sixteen inches taller than me. He took that opportunity to sneeze, covering my military-green coat in what I imagined was military-green mucus.

Apologetically shaking his head, he pointed to a few piles of dirt at the front door. "Dusty," he intoned sagely.

Gross. Super gross.

"No worries," I said with a forced grin. "Maybe they fired the maid, and this was revenge, eh?"

The orc frowned for a beat before amusement lit up his eyes. He chucked his head back and laughed loudly.

I adjusted my jacket around my shoulders. I would probably need to have the thing incinerated. Orcs carried gnarly germs.

Nodding my goodbye, I walked into the main hallway, sidestepping the sandy mess at the door.

I needed to talk to Eros, my contact inside Warden. Julia had four Sentinels assigned to her. Nothing should have been able to get to her.

Twisting my call-stone—a device that resembled a polished black ring—around the middle finger of my right hand, I waited until I felt the prickle of magic to picture Eros in my mind. It was basically a phone that transmitted live video, but I found it harder to break than human devices.

The ring was an expensive little gadget, but I could afford it. Playing in politics was lucrative if one knew how to properly balance. I did a fair job of it, but it didn't hurt that my family was titled and wealthy.

I was a Draconian through my father. Apparently, someone on my paternal side had diddled a dragon in human form, and so many generations later, the resulting spawn had diddled my mother—a fairly well-known succubus who might have traded a few favors of a carnal nature for the powers of a sorceress. It left me part empath, part succubus, and wholly unable to get a blouse that fit my wide shoulders.

Dad's scaly DNA carried a lot of clout—and a few anger-management issues. After a slightly cataclysmic accident as a child, I was taken to a witch doctor to have my Spark sealed. You destroy a few city blocks, and everyone loses their minds. The witch doctor had taken my Spark and put its essence into a pretty pendant that I wore at all times. I couldn't access it, though. My mother had it locked so that it only responded to her touch.

Mom, a prominent figurehead in the Royal House, occasionally tried to upset Parliament and grapple control for herself. She came close when I was younger, and I still got my share of side-eyes when I walked into a room.

Parliament had split from the Royal House not too many years back due to infighting and power struggles. They both operated as the unified governing body of the fae, but the balancing act between the two was a hard thing to manage. The Royal House still resented having power taken from them, and Parliament was always trying to suck more.

Eros, Operations for Warden, finally responded to my call.

"Kass?" he asked, grinning when he saw my face projected through our rings.

Normally, I would have been flattered if a man smiled upon seeing my face, but Eros was well versed in flattery.

"Hey, Ross. Got a min?" I asked. Calling him Eros seemed awfully grandiose. I had known the man for centuries and considered him a trusted friend.

"Only for you," he said with a wink.

Ross was exceedingly attractive, but most vampires were. Not due to genetics altering their genome, but because vampires had their own brand of glamour that kept them movie-star pretty.

It was a predator thing. Attractive people could approach you in the dark. They could invite themselves into your home, ask for a ride in a dark alley. We were programmed to be less suspicious of ravishing individuals.

"I need a list of the Sentinels posted to Julia," I said without much preamble. I normally took a few minutes to flirt with the fanged hottie, but I didn't really have time for it today.

Ross frowned at me. "Why?" he asked, curiosity obvious in his voice.

I shrugged, my jacket stretching across my shoulders. "She's dead."

Ross cursed loudly.

"Yeah, it's a mess. No sign of the Sentinels."

I could hear Ross clicking his tongue against his teeth at the implication.

Sentinels were sacred. As children, they were given to the Warden program, which trained them to be lethal, dogged, and humorless—perfect soldiers. It was rare that someone—or something—got past them without losing an eye or two.

Either the Sentinels were given an order to allow someone inside, or they complied of their own volition. Neither looked good for Warden . . . or Ross, who headed the program.

I watched the dark-haired man walk out of his office and into a brightly lit stairwell before exiting through a roof-access door. He lowered his voice to a whisper.

"Who's with you?"

I shrugged. "I came alone, but the cleaning crew was already at it. Trillby called me in."

He twisted his lips in thought. "We need to discuss a few things."

"Ross, are you involved in this mess?" I asked wearily. Ross was clever and connected, but that didn't mean he was infallible.

"No, but I think I know who is." Abruptly looking up from the call, he muttered, "Seek Solace." Then he hung up.

"What the actual hell?" I grumbled, closing my hand into a fist around call-stone. The headache I'd been trying to stave off decided it was there to stay and throbbed annoyingly against my temples to the tune of a German metal song.

Not to be horribly stereotypical, but vampires could be tiresome. They so enjoyed their subterfuge. Ross obviously had a bead on what was going on, but he had left me in the dark and given me a cryptic message instead of anything worthwhile.

I shrugged. It sounded like most of my dates, really.

"He's where?"

Ross's secretary stared at me with bored, lackluster eyes. "Gone for the day."

"The head of Warden just decided to take the rest of the day off?" I asked sarcastically, not expecting a reply.

His face was emotionless as he nodded. Being empathic might have sounded like such a nifty trick, but I only used it when I was cheating at board games. As a general rule, people were terrifically easy to read.

"You don't know where he would've gone, do you?" I asked with a cheery smile that didn't do anything to ease my headache or my annoyance.

"Nope." He added a terse "Sorry" after I scowled.

"May I leave him a note?" I replied, pressing my thumb against my temple.

"Name?" he asked, taking out a pen.

"Lord High Steward Kassandra Tatsu," I said softly, taking it as a small victory when his eyes lit up in recognition.

Ross's secretary, who promptly introduced himself as Ian, apologized for the delay and handed me a sealed envelope.

"I was given express orders to hand this to you personally," Ian said rather self-importantly.

"From Ross?" I asked, taking the paper.

"Yes, ma'am. I mean, Your Lordship. Your Ladyship?"

I flicked a long nail under the edge of the envelope and ripped it open, taking a moment of pleasure in having Ian grovel.

"Kass will suffice, I would think," I said graciously.

Pulling out a sheet of light-blue paper, I fought to keep confusion from seeping into my expression. It was blank. Was something scrawled in invisible ink? Or did it require some other spectrum of light that I wasn't able to see? Maybe the thing was enchanted.

Maybe Ross was screwing with me because it was in his genes to play with his food.

"This is it? No verbal message to go along with it?"

"No, Your Lady—Kass. He just told me I should give you this and you would know what to do with it."

Did Ross think I had just shared a bed with Sherlock and could suddenly decipher codes from thin air?

I nodded in thanks and walked back to my mirror-black car. I wasn't overly versed in technical jargon regarding vehicles, but I did love a nice mirror glaze.

I glanced at the paper again, half hoping something would appear if I were by myself.

There was nothing save a tiny red poppy watermark on the corner of the paper. To the right of the flower was an address for a posh bar called Solace.

Seek Solace.

What a load of crap.

Leave it to a vampire to be an absolute pain in the neck.

*R*oss and I were fairly close; otherwise, I would have handed this over to Parliament and been on my merry way. Personally, I found it terminally stupid to get involved with things that had the potential to land me on the wrong side of whoever was in power.

As it was, I pulled up to Solace, parked almost legally, and made my way through the fairly nondescript entrance. Bright lights and shoji screens guided me into the main room.

To my left, a woman bowed and greeted me in a language I was unfamiliar with. It could have been Japanese, but I wasn't positive.

"Eros?" I asked, my eyebrows shooting up in question.

She smiled, bowed again, and beckoned me toward an arched door I hadn't noticed upon entering the bar.

"*Erabu, dozo*," she said, bowing me through the doorway.

The room she led me into was spartan but cozy. Tatami mats lined the floor, and a massive stick of incense burned quietly in the corner.

"Manto will see you," she said in a heavy accent. "I am Pythia. Please summon me if you have need of anything."

I need you to tell me what in the seventh circle of Hades is going on, I thought uncharitably.

"Pythia cannot answer your questions," said a lovely dark-haired woman who stood at a large window.

Fae could use magic on one another, but it was a fairly restricted practice as it was beyond rude. I pulled a face in annoyance. I didn't care to have my thoughts intruded upon.

"Apologies," Manto murmured, ducking her head in embarrassment. "I remember all time; it isn't linear for me."

Oh, good. An oracle.

If I left now, I could grab dinner and be home in plenty of time for a bath. I would also miss out on figuring out what Ross was embroiled in.

"Please, *dozo*," she said, gesturing to a large flat pillow in front of the low window.

Like the absolute and complete idiot I was, I complied.

As I sat, I asked, "What is an *Erabu?*"

"You," Manto said with a blooming smile.

I raised an eyebrow. Any normal person would follow that up with an explanation, but not an oracle. They were basically vision-having cats who liked to knock things off desks and play with defenseless animals.

"*Meaning?*"

"Chosen."

Dear gods. Sentences, lady, speak in full sentences. "For what?" I questioned aloud.

"The prophecy," she said, stringing two whole words together.

"You think I am mentioned in a prophecy?" I asked, pronouncing every word as if she were too softheaded to understand.

"Oh, yes," she said with a nod. "You are dragonkin, daughter of the Power Seeker. You will bring peace for four hundred years."

"Peace to what?" I inquired, letting curiosity get the better of me.

"To the fae, Kassandra. United in brotherhood for centuries."

I frowned. The history of my people was a bloodied one. No more than the human world, I suppose, except we threw fireballs instead of cannonballs.

"Are we not at peace now?" I shrugged and added, "Ignoring the few coups my mother has led."

Manto tilted her head to the right. "We are on the verge of a centuries-long war that would wipe us from history. Only handfuls would remain."

"The humans?" I asked, wondering if they would be affected.

"The war would be impossible to hide from them."

"To be clear, this doesn't involve a virginal sacrifice, does it?" I asked with a smirk, reminding myself that I wasn't fully invested in oracles or visions.

She looked confused for a moment, her eyes losing their focus. "You've already stopped the sacrifices."

What the what?

Talking to an oracle was like trying to unravel a knot of wet rope with frozen fingers during a hurricane. It hurt, it was frustrating, and it was mostly futile. Everything I would do, this woman saw as something I had already done. So apparently, at some point, I save people from being sacrificed.

High five to my future self.

The dark-haired woman reached out to take my arm. Her mocha fingers hovered just above my skin, waiting for permission to touch me.

Oracle-induced visions were not fun, so I hesitated. The normal mind balked at having memories of future events shoved into its synapses.

Also, they made absolutely no sense. The swishy mist of incomplete pictures that only made sense after the fact tended to give me more of a headache than any actual action points. My mother had always fancied them, though.

Fae legend held that the original oracles were daughters of Apollo. Generations of diluted blood kept the daughters from fully seeing future events but allowed them partial access to their heritage. It's why we allowed the barbaric practice of keeping oracles virgins until a blood-match was found for breeding.

The fae didn't want their soothsayers to lose the ability of seeing the future—even if it was in fits and starts.

Cursing, I agreed to let Manto wrap her long fingers around my forearm.

Upon her touch, my brain felt as if tiny cleated ants were marching to war over it, but eventually it allowed me to see the information it was being force-fed.

A great behemoth stirred underground—hungry, demanding.

A handshake flashed gold and purple. Babies cried. A softly shifting desert.

An explosion bloomed behind my eyelids. People screamed in pain. Someone was laughing.

When my poor skull couldn't take the pain any longer, I wrenched my arm loose from Manto's grip. I proceeded to collapse against the windowsill, where I lay curled in a fetal position until the smell of bergamot made me look up.

Pythia knelt beside me, holding a blue cup under my nose.

"Tea will help, *Erabu*," she insisted.

I pushed myself up on my elbows and happily accepted the warm cup of fragrant herbs and flowers.

"What was that . . . thing?" I croaked out, referring to the giant shadow I had seen shifting in the vision.

"Dolos," Manto offered. "He is crafty."

"Well, what does he want?" Greed and deceit had radiated off the massive beast in great shimmering waves. Fantastic attributes to have when he was large enough to swallow a bus.

"He already has what he wants. He is no threat."

"No threat?" I replied, trying to stand. "He is treachery personified." *Also, thanks so much for stuffing that image in my head when it was worthless.*

"Dolos has been fed; Dolos will starve. Hidden handshakes will come to light. The great fire must rage. Peace will come." Manto stared past me into nothingness.

I clicked my tongue against the roof of my mouth and nodded, instantly regretting it. "Well, that's helpful," I said, cross with today's events and sounding a bit petulant, even to my own ears.

I turned my attention to Pythia. "Can you enlighten me at all?"

"I am merely an acolyte, *Erabu*. I have no gifts."

"I'm assuming she won't be able to carry on much of a conversation now," I said, motioning toward Manto. The oracle was mumbling to herself and tracing small patterns in the air.

Pythia nodded solemnly. "She must rest."

I tossed back the rest of the tea. "I don't suppose you can tell me where Eros is?"

"In hiding," she replied in her silky accent.

"From whom?" I asked, wondering who the head of Warden could possibly need to hide from.

"Your mother," Pythia said, before turning her attention wholly to her master.

Of course, my mother sent me to voicemail when I reached out to her on with the call-stone. She was probably busy taking over a small fiefdom.

My only other option was to head to Parliament to meet her in person, but I couldn't go in my current attire. There was a fairly strict dress code. It was unwritten, but I wouldn't even get through the door in my current getup.

I felt my shoulders sag in relaxation as I walked through the arched door of my gray-and-white flat.

A massive fluffy black-and-gray cat peeked one eye open to stare at me before it decided I wasn't worth the effort and closed it again.

"Nice to see you too," I groused lovingly. I wasn't huge on pets, but Gizmo was excellent as far as non-needy fuzz balls went. She didn't sleep with me, sneeze on me, or sit on my laptop. She did, however, love death metal, leaving me alone, and occasionally squeaking the cutest meow known to Earth.

Mom had sent her to me as an olive branch the last time she roused the rabble into revolt. I'm fairly sure she used Giz to spy on me, but I didn't really care overly much. I guess it's kind of sweet in a demented "my mother is an overlord" sort of way.

Taking off my boots, I set them in their respective cubby in front of the door. I don't understand why anyone would wear street shoes inside their home. Shoes spend hours treading over chewing gum, spit, snot, blood, and various other disgusting fluids. To blithely smudge that horror-show cocktail across the floor one later walks barefoot on is cognitive dissonance at its finest.

After depositing my footwear, I slipped on a cozy pair of white slippers that could have been Gizmo's cousins before walking into my bedroom and undressing.

I should have gone straight to sleep to stave off the vision-headache, but I needed to process the shovelsful of crazy that Manto had tossed my way.

I'm not sure what my mother had to do with any of this, but it was nothing good if she was involved. And why was Ross hiding from her? The vampire could take care of himself, but if he had somehow crossed Mom . . .

As I shrugged into a slinky silver dress that weighed far too much, I managed to stub my toe on a zen garden Giz had apparently knocked off my dresser.

I stopped short of yelling at the devilish fuzz ball as I remembered the piles of dust at the front of Julia's apartment.

My mouth popped open.

There had been sand in the vision Manto had shared with me.

Throwing on the ornate mantle that matched my dress, I called Trillby as I ran out the front door.

***

"It's what?" I asked, confusion causing my brows to knit together.

"Residue from a destroyed golem," Rachael repeated in her polite monotone voice. "Mostly sand, but it's a very particular type. Like a skin cell, but for a golem."

I paused to rub the silt between my fingers. Golems weren't something I ran into on a regular basis. "Like a statue?" I asked her stupidly.

She nodded, her high ponytail bobbing. "A shapeless, mindless being, given form and function by whoever created it."

"Are they dangerous?" I asked, wondering why the hell there would have been golems at the front of Julia's apartment.

The tech shrugged. "Not unless the creator wants them to be. They are simply a vessel for intentions."

"Huh," I said out loud. Had someone created a golem to take out Julia? If so, why leave the evidence at the crime scene?

"How are they destroyed?"

"They are very structurally sound," she commented, her eyes lighting up at the chance to explain something she found fascinating. "But they can be destroyed easily if someone knows where the Fingerprint of Creation is located."

"Assume I do not know what that is," I said with a toothy grin.

"It is literally the fingerprint of the creator upon the golem, and the weakest point on the creature. If struck, the golem will crumble. Old kings used golems as guards until this was discovered."

"So they could potentially be used as assassins?" I mused aloud.

Rachael nodded. "Small jobs might be fit for golems, but it would be purely nonsensical to create an army from them. The moment someone found them out, they could easily be destroyed."

My brain fizzled with half-baked thoughts. Could someone have sent golems to attack Julia and her entourage? But then, why would someone make a golem for it to only come to the crime scene anyway?

This detective stuff was not working for me. I soothed the hurt feelings of fae that ran the government. I didn't find murderers.

"How close does one need to be to control a golem?" I asked.

The woman leaned forward. "It doesn't work like that. Once the golem is instilled with its purpose, it can operate independently until death."

I thanked the tech for her time and left for Parliament with zero answers.

I needed a magic eight ball.

T he parliamentary building was ridiculous. The massive gothic castle was a work of sheer wonder, but it was still ridiculous. It floated over the human city, domed in a purple glamour only fae could see. Employees, guests, and dignitaries had to be teleported by magi. Parliament claimed it was for security reasons, but we all knew it was for show.

Glistening hallways formed of veined marble and crystal were illuminated from within. Gilded arches supported transparent crystal domes that allowed the light of the crescent moon to spill in.

An unsmiling Sentinel escorted me to my mother's office, his blank expression making me uneasy. Sentinel training had always creeped me out a bit, as not much was known about it. It was considered an honor to give your child into service and was a way for poor families to climb rank, but it smacked of selling your kids for social status. Parliament used Sentinels as a sort of specialized army, however, so there was no way they would stop touting the righteousness of placing one's children into the care of the government.

Falling into habit, I concentrated that fuzzy empathic tendril that floated like an invisible flyaway above my head on the Sentinel walking beside me . . . and felt nothing, really. In some cases with Sentinels, the mind I reached out to touch would be so determined and strong-willed that I would only get the repetition of one or a few words instead of a general feeling of emotion. This Sentinel's was "protect."

He must be an absolute blast to converse with.

"I'll be in the hallway to take you back, ma'am," he said with a terse smile.

I nodded before entering the red-toned office where my mother spent a good deal of her time. I walked into the room, expecting to take a seat, but stopped short upon noticing Caesar sitting behind my mother's desk.

Confused, I quickly bowed, hand over my heart, a pledge of fealty one made when working for Parliament.

"Steward Kassandra," he said with his own formal bow. "To what do I owe the honor of your visit?"

Here, I was meant to spend twenty minutes talking about the mundane: family, land holdings, and—particular to Caesar—any new spells he had managed to learn. However, if Caesar learned I had spent time babbling and bantering for half an hour while I withheld from him the death of his consort, he would have me flayed.

Where the short lives of humans made them laconic and ungracious, the long lives of fae made us wordy and banal.

Still confused as to why the head of Parliament would be on speaking terms with a woman who was constantly trying to usurp him, I fairly stuttered, "I am sorry to say I have news that would preclude pleasantries."

The tall elf stood, his ceremonial cloak settling around him like a living thing. "Oh?" he said, almost uneasily.

Steeling myself, as I was about to commit suicide politically and possibly literally, I slowly said, "Julia, niece of Orilius, is dead." I paused, unsure if I should add that she had been brutally slain. "Murdered, it seems," I added softly.

The air slowly leaked from Caesar's lithe form. His regal bearing wilted as I watched.

"Julia?"

I nodded, biting my lip in a nervous habit that prevented me from playing card games.

"I had four Sentinels at her door." He paused briefly. "But I suppose they have gone?" he asked quietly, raising his hand to his chest.

Why would he assume that?

"No sign of them. I believe someone had golems perform the attack. There was evidence of golem remains at the door."

Walking stoically around my mother's room, the prime minister perched himself on an ornate chair. His eyes seemed to lose their light.

Caesar was devastated . . . and drowning in guilt.

He again lifted his hand to his chest, as if his heart were failing. A flash of purple and gold reflected off his large signet ring and into my eyes.

My head felt like someone had cracked a watermelon over it, and the pain almost dropped me to my knees.

The visions Manto had shared with me bounced around in my skull like a ball made of metal spikes. Flashbacks tended to hurt more than the original visions, as they were not being shared with the oracle.

A handshake.

One hand had been large, brown, and bumpy; the other had been smooth, tan, and decorated with a gold-and-purple ring. Exactly like the one Caesar was wearing.

"Dolos," I muttered.

Caesar's jaw tightened before he locked eyes with me. "Who?" he asked carefully.

I could feel he was lying, of course. I was a walking lie detector, and people still tried to speak mistruths around me. Hubris and all that.

"You made a deal with that monstrosity?" I demanded, shocked to my core. "What did you offer Dolos in return for Julia?" I asked, my heart slamming against my ribs almost painfully.

"Not Julia," he said, a catch in his voice. "I would never have hurt her."

"Caesar, what have you done?" I asked. "That creature is vile. He cannot be trusted."

Caesar stood, anger coming off him in almost visible waves.

"I did *not* have Julia killed," he hissed at me, slashing his hand through the air. He was still devastated, but it didn't seem to stem from the death of his consort.

"They were there to *protect* her," Caesar said, almost under his breath.

"Who? The Sentinels?"

Fine job they did of that.

"Yes, the twice-cursed Sentinels."

"Then why order them away?" I asked, confused.

"No one sent the Sentinels away, you silly girl. They never left."

I listened to the thrum of my heart for three beats before I understood.

"The piles of dust at the front door—they were the Sentinels?" My voice trembled with the gut punch of realization.

"Golems are meant to be indestructible," he muttered.

I shook my head. "There is a mark on them—the Fingerprint of Creation—that allows people to easily turn them to dust. That is why they fell out of favor for armies centuries ago."

"Do you think I would have used them if I had known that?" Caesar asked with more condescension than I cared for.

Why would Caesar replace the Sentinels with something he knew so little about?

"What does Dolos have to do with this?" I asked, wondering what sort of deal Caesar could have struck with the demigod.

The elegant creature shrugged, as if settling into his fate. Lowering his voice, the elf lord said, "We give him children. He gives us Sentinels. They were meant to be indestructible, to give us an edge against your horrible mother's schemes to take over Parliament!"

I swore loudly, a punishable offense when done in front of the prime minister.

"You've replaced all the Sentinels with golems?" I whispered, almost sick to my stomach. "What happens to the children, Caesar?" I questioned, my heart sinking into my knees.

"Dolos must be fed," he said meekly, mirroring something Manto had muttered hours ago.

"Gods, no. How many?" I demanded softly, my chest tightening against the atrocity of giving our own children to a devouring beast.

The elf lord lowered his head for a moment before snapping back into his rigid posture. "It had to be done. Can't you see that? We had to be protected from your mother!"

"She cannot possibly be that much of a threat that you would feed children to a monster!" I cried, still shattered by the realization of what had been happening.

Caesar chuckled. "Did you know that I wanted to use you to get to her? My staff advised me against it. You've done much to separate yourself from that woman, and they doubted you would be of any use at all. It seems they were correct."

I flared my nostrils in indignation. "She's done her fair share of pillaging. I wouldn't have a career if I maintained a relationship with her."

"She's been threatening to take back power from Parliament," he said angrily. He looked down his straight nose at me. "I suppose this was her way of getting my attention."

"By killing your consort?" I asked, aghast. I knew Parliament and the Royal House were forever at odds, but I had never taken the time to think about the boggy details of what went on behind the scenes.

"She's been conspiring to take over Parliament for ages, Kassandra. We thought the Sentinels could stop her. A deal was struck with Dolos. We gave him the children slated for Warden, and he gave us golems as Sentinels."

I swallowed twice before responding. "Is Eros involved?"

I could handle my estranged mother and the prime minister losing themselves to greed, but not someone I broke bread with.

Caesar shook his head. "How should I know?" he asked almost scathingly. "This is a disaster."

"If my mother finds out that Parliament has no army . . ." I said, my brain shifting to the prophecy Manto had mentioned. "Caesar, if she finds out, there will be a war that decimates the fae. It cannot come to fighting, or we will be *annihilated.*"

"I took these measures to avoid a war," he said with a hiss.

"Caesar, how did you find out about Dolos?" I asked, my skin buzzing.

He turned to answer, his mouth opening and then snapping shut like a suffocating fish's. "There was a gift on my desk. A book. It held information on Dolos and his favors."

"From whom?" I asked softly.

"There wasn't a name."

I swallowed twice.

My mother knew.

She *knew* the Sentinels were golems. She *knew* I would reach out to Ross. She *knew* I would seek the oracle.

This was all my mother's doing from the start. She had woven a web and watched as we all tumbled headfirst into the sticky thing.

Caesar was useless. He blamed himself for Julia's death, but he would not surrender to my mother when the time came . . . and the time would come. She had patiently played the long game with all of us, skillfully moving us around and waiting until we fell into line.

She had always wanted to rule, but not just one section of the fae government; she wanted it all. She wanted absolute power and would stop at nothing—not even annihilation—to get it.

If, as I suspected, my mother knew about the prophecy, I wasn't sure why she hadn't simply done away with me. Or did she think I would find it in my heart to serve her cause because we had a blood tie?

I ran down the marble-and-crystal hallway, my brain buzzing with other people's spinning emotions. An alert was blasting through Parliament; they were prepping for battle.

I needed to find my gods-cursed mother. If I could convince Caesar to surrender to her terms, we may be able to broker a four-hundred-year peace.

A tough thing to swallow, surrender, but it sounded miles better than an all-out decimation.

Skidding around a corner, I tried to stop too quickly and half tumbled over a woman dressed in red-and-black robes so encrusted with jewels, they had to be enchanted for her to even stand. A tumble of raven-black hair fell in shining waves down her back.

She arched a perfect brow in my direction. "I have always liked seeing you in silver." She paused and smiled prettily. "You could have made an effort with your hair, however."

"Hi, Mother. Here to wipe out all faekind?" I asked with all the sarcasm I could shove into the two little sentences. Mom and I weren't friends, but she was a force of nature and I had to respect that.

She tsked at me, her mouth pulling down into a pout. "No, Kassandra. I am here to have you stand for me. We have a meeting with the Speaker in Parliament Hall."

"You could have just called me back," I said testily.

"You never answer," she chastised with a small smile. "Your father has tainted your opinion of me, I'm afraid."

Of course she would turn it around and make it my fault. She was gifted at snaking conversations around until you were too twisted to know which direction was up.

"You blew up an entire underground city," I said, beginning to tick her dastardly deeds off on my fingers. "You wiped out a tribe of people during peace talks, and—oh, yeah!—you had the leader of Parliament feed *children* to a monster . . . and that was all *this* year!" I hissed, my voice going up several octaves by the end.

My mother rolled her beautiful sage-blue eyes. "Don't be dramatic, Kassandra. Caesar made his own choices."

I briefly wondered what decisions Eros had made to land him in this mess before I realized my mistake. My mother's eyes lit up.

I snapped my mind shut to my mother. "That was incredibly rude," I barked, incensed she had prodded around in my head. "Did you kill him?" I may have sounded flippant, but losing a centuries-long friend to my mother would likely cause a break in our already bumpy relationship.

"Of course not," she said, pulling her brows together into a frown. "He found out about the Sentinels too early, and I had to force him into hiding. He has gone to Bavaria."

"He wasn't involved?"

"Only in that he was too enamored of his own reflection to see what was happening."

"And Julia?"

My mother's eyes flashed in annoyance. "Honestly, darling, if I had known you were going to be so upset about everything, I would have gone about it quite differently."

"Liar."

She shrugged her slim shoulders. "Julia was poised to go public about us to the humans. It served two purposes to have her done away with."

"Then why leave evidence that the Sentinels were actually golems?" I asked, curiosity getting the better of me.

My mother marched down the halls of Parliament as if she owned it—granted, she probably would in a few hours. She looked like an empress of old preparing for battle. Her red robes billowed out behind her like the fire of a phoenix's tail.

"Like I said, you never take my calls," she replied shortly.

"You left evidence as bait?" I asked, so dumbfounded that I actually stopped walking for a moment. I had to jog to catch back up with her.

I could manipulate people with the best of them, but convincing an entire branch of government to cede power to my mother seemed a bit of a stretch.

I was missing something vital, and I knew my mother wasn't going to be forthcoming about it.

As my mother and I stood in Parliament Hall, I watched the leaders of my people slowly gather. Their outfits were decked out in precious metals and jewels, and even now, even on the eve of what could be their decimation, they vied for position and rank. They shouldered past those they thought were lesser and raised their voices to be heard, especially when they had nothing to say.

Caesar confessed to his dealings with Dolos, but as none in Parliament had children that had been eaten by the great monster, the only concern came from having a diminished army.

My head swam with sorrow and anger. I reeled in my empathic feeler and shut my brain off from the suffocating crowd of privileged speakers.

None of them cared.

They looked upon the deaths of hundreds of children with a shrug.

Their worry was for themselves.

When the time came for my mother to speak, she looked at me with a sad smile. "I need to borrow your necklace, Kassandra."

Heat bloomed where my necklace touched my throat. And then I understood.

My job was not to influence or cajole. It was to literally light the fire of a centuries-long war. One that would lead to four hundred years of the fae being united in peaceful brotherhood.

The war would decimate our numbers, our prejudices, and our caste system. The small pockets remaining would form a terrified alliance for generations.

Only on the brink of extinction could we be at peace.

Meeting her terrible, beautiful eyes, I nodded in understanding before handing her the silver-and-green necklace that contained my Spark.

I heard my mother laughing as I walked out of the room. The sound of an explosion followed close behind.

HIDDEN DEMONS

Ben Collins

*S*ome students opened their test packets and stared in horror, as they had expected the test to be a simple set of multiple-choice questions and had chosen not to prepare. Others got to work, knowing they would do all right, neither amazing nor awful.

Then there was John. He opened his packet with a smile, as he knew he just needed to complete twenty minutes of random passages to maintain his A and then he would have a week of spring break to relax and ignore any thoughts of the concrete prison he sat in.

As the test continued, John looked around to see the other students become more and more distraught as they realized how much their grades would fall. Some were constantly flipping their papers; others were tapping their pencils faster than a jackhammer. All the terms and stories they had ignored for an entire semester had returned with a terrible vengeance, seemingly with the sole purpose of tanking their averages. Amid the flurry of tapping pencils and fluttering papers, John stood with a wide grin, walked over to Mr. Wissen's desk, and slammed his test down.

"Once you set your test down, you can't take it back. Are you sure you want to turn it in? You still have more than an hour and a half left," Mr. Wissen warned, looking over the top of his glasses.

"Nah, I'm good. If I don't know it already, I won't in five minutes." John beamed before he turned and walked out of the class and to the cafeteria.

Once there, he sat down at the usual place and took out his favorite book to read for the sixth time.

After thirty minutes, John felt a tap on his shoulder and looked up to see Blake drop down in the chair next to him.

"Hope you weren't waiting too long; the physics midterm was *brutal,* so I needed to check over a couple of answers." Blake leaned back in his chair, cracking his back. "The exam was almost just electricity and light. You really should study for it. A couple of the formulas weren't on the formula sheet."

"When I study, it always does more harm than good, so I'll pass on that. Thanks for the heads up, though," John said.

Daniel dropped down at their table.

"Hey, SlevetiestLime is here!" John cracked. He tried to stifle his amusement at Daniel's original screen name, but he wasn't quite successful.

"How many times do I have to tell you? I didn't choose the stupid name; the computer did! What if I kept calling you by your original name, ToxicMaster? That's even worse since you chose it!" Daniel quipped back.

John visibly cringed at the mention of his seventh-grade "genius."

"At ease, you two; save it for the bosses," Justin called from the hallway.

"There's our wonderful leader!" quipped John. "Hey, Justin, took you long enough. Weren't you in the stat test? You know, that class is designed to help people graduate." John smirked.

Justin sneered. "I fell asleep, like, five minutes after it was handed out. When I woke up, I did it in ten. Fight me."

"At ease, Chief; save it for the bosses," John mocked. "So what made you guys finally decide to take me up on my offer to start playing? I don't think I've said anything extraordinary recently."

"Well, with spring break starting, we have a week to decide if we really like it. So why not try now?" Blake answered.

ith a wide grin, John rushed home and spent hours exploring the sides of mountains, deep caves, a couple of wandering merchants, and even a towering volcano to get materials, potions, and equipment for everyone to use. Seven o'clock rolled around, and no one else was online.

"Maybe I just missed a message," John thought aloud, opening the group chat. Nothing.

Maybe it was the other chat?

Pulling up his social media, John was flooded with pictures of his friends together at a party. It looked like every single person from school was behind them, smiling and laughing.

Maybe they just forgot to tell me about it. John started to panic. *But why would they spend an hour planning to play if they were going to a party?*

Trying to figure out where the communication had dropped, John sent a message to each of them individually and then to the group chat.

They all read the messages within half an hour, but no one responded. The little eye icon that indicated the messages had been seen and ignored taunted him from the bottom of the chat. He sat staring at his screen for another fifteen minutes, hoping they had just got caught up in a conversation and were about to say something, *anything,* to him, even the most basic and apathetic "Sorry, dude." John waited until two in the morning before he received another notification.

It was just another post on Daniel's page.

"Tonight was awesome. All my favorite people were here. Sad it had to end, but that just means we can have another party later today XD."

After waiting another half hour, staying awake just on hope, John had had enough. He plugged his phone in and threw himself on the bed. He was asleep before his head even hit the pillow.

John's night was filled with tossing, turning, and horrible dreams.

Dreams where he was a fly on the wall, listening to his friends list all the things they didn't like about him.

Then another dream, where they formed a circle around him.

Justin glared down at him. "You only read or play video games. Why would anyone actually be your friend?"

"You never want to do anything fun, like go to a theme park or go rock climbing."

John's dreams devolved from there, turning more and more into anger at himself for not being more like his friends and preferring quiet to parties. After several minutes, instead of just being told why no one liked him, he started imagining his friends physically attacking him, all the while degrading him and telling him why he was worthless.

He snapped awake just before the dream versions of his friends could kick him simultaneously. The morning sun, peeking through his window, momentarily blinded him as he slowly processed the dreams he had had.

"What was that, brain? They skipped one event; that doesn't mean they hate me. I'm overreacting, just like in middle school," John said, trying to reassure himself.

He slowly lumbered out of bed and downstairs to the kitchen, where his cats were staring at their food bowl. He flipped on the lights, gaining the attention of the two cats, Nemo and Tina. They rushed over and rubbed their heads against his leg.

"Good to see you two still like me, though I think you just like me because I bring you food."

As if to answer him, Nemo let out a small meow, looking back at the food bowl.

"All right, all right, I'm on it."

John grabbed the food bag and the cup he used as a shovel. Just as he was about to pour some in, he saw the bowl was still more than half-full.

"What the heck, you two? Don't act like I haven't fed you in weeks when there is still half a bowl left! Is it just on the wrong side? What? Neither of you will eat out of the fabled far side?"

Instead of refilling their bowl, he just shook it around so that the piled-up food leveled out and shifted to the "correct side." Before John could set the dish back down, Nemo was bounding over anything in her way to get to the food she had ignored only moments ago.

"Why are you so weird, cat?"

"Morning, Son. They probably get it from their owner," his dad joked. "Do you know where the cast-iron skillet went? I want to make a couple of pancakes before I head to work, and I don't know where I put it last."

"I put it in the cabinet to the left of the sink. Unless the cats can suddenly lift cast iron, it should still be there," John replied. "Since I knew where it was, can you make me one too, please?"

"You also moved it, so it's your fault I didn't know where it went. But sure, you can have one, if you grab me the mix out of the pantry."

"You drive a hard bargain, old man, but deal."

"You keep calling me old, and Christmas dinner is going to be replaced with kale smoothies and salads," he quipped.

"You wouldn't!" John gasped in anguish. "You like actual food just as much as I do! You would never do that to yourself just to spite me!"

"You're forgetting that I can drive to places with actual food, instead of just being stuck here like you are," Mr. Smith retorted with a wide smirk. "Hurry up and hand me the mix, or I'm going to be late."

"Yes, sir!"

John bolted to the pantry and skimmed every shelf until he found it. Just as he was about to hand the mix to his dad, he heard his phone ring from his room and ran off to check it. The muffled thud of the mix bottle falling to the floor could be heard.

In his hurry out of the kitchen, John didn't hear it or his dad calling his name with a hint of growing anger in his voice. He was fully focused on seeing if one of his friends said anything about last night.

John dove onto his bed and ripped his phone off the charger, only to see that the notification had just been an app announcing it had automatically updated. After a slow trudge back to the kitchen, John heard a foot tapping. After seeing why, his face went as red as the Chinese flag.

"Care to explain yourself?" Mr. Smith asked, not bothering to hide the anger in his voice.

"U-um, well, I've been waiting for one of my friends to respond, and I thought that ding was them, so I went to check it. I'm sorry."

Mr. Smith sighed. "Well, I don't think we have enough mix to make multiple, so your punishment will be to clean this and not get one."

"Again, I am really sorry," John mumbled, grabbing the broom from the pantry.

The kitchen soon filled with the smell and sizzle of the cooking pancake, which caused John's stomach to make a noise that rivaled the trumpets of the seventh seal.

Spring break continued, and John became more and more reclusive. The more days that passed, the more he stayed in his room, the less he ate at the table, and the less he talked to anyone.

By Monday, he would just grab the smallest bit of food and take it back to eat in complete silence. He forwent any music, TV, or games to read the same two books over and over. The occasional thought flashed through his mind: *Can you really blame them for ditching you? They never cared about playing the game, so why would now be different?*

By Wednesday, he was skipping food entirely and spent all day staring at his messages app, even though nothing ever showed up. His dad would periodically check in on him, trying to get him to eat something or at least come out of his room, but to no avail. The intrusive thoughts were more prevalent and common.

You've seen them roll their eyes every time you spend an hour talking about some small detail that even the devs forgot about. They probably saw an easy out and jumped on it in a heartbeat. Maybe they won't come back; it would be an easy jumping-away point, a break that is also a break from you that lasts forever.

On Thursday morning, he woke up, checked his phone, saw there were still no notifications, and went back to sleep for four hours. For the entire day, he was never awake for more than thirty seconds at a time, and he was awake for less than three minutes the entire day. His attempt to push away his thoughts by sleeping turned out to be much worse than if he had been awake, as he was stuck in his own mind, alone with his own personal demons.

Get over yourself. Actually important people wouldn't be distraught this long. They'd have their day of "The world is ending, woe is me!" and it would be over. Why do you think you're so special as to need a whole week to get over some people? Oh boo-hoo, your friends stopped talking to you for five days. Better call the National Guard to see if they are even alive! Be a functional human for once in your life and move on.

I'm sure they did before they ever got to the party. I mean, did you see Daniel's post?

"All my favorite people . . ."

"All my favorite people . . ."

"Every person I actually want to talk to even the slightest bit *is here!*"

But where were you again? That's right, sitting at home, on your computer, by yourself. I'm sure that put things in a new light. I really can't blame them. If you're like this every time something goes the slightest bit wrong, I would have dumped you on the side of the road the second time something happened. Heaven forbid you scrape your knee or something. I bet you could solve all the water problems with your tears if you did.

Do everyone a favor and just keep to yourself and keep your mouth shut.

Friday's sun was well above the horizon when John woke up at nine. As had become his routine, John checked his phone one last time to still see no messages from any—

Blake just responded! John's face lit up like the Pope's Christmas tree.

Blake: Dude, I am so sorry I couldn't respond earlier. My mom found out I was at that party and grounded me for the entire break. Apparently, my sister doesn't bluff when she says she'll blackmail me. She said she wanted the keys to my car for a week since I'm not supposed to go to Catherine's house, and when I didn't give in, she ratted me out to my mom. I knew you wouldn't want to go to the party too because it was a bunch of loud people in one house. I still should have let you know what happened, though. I am so sorry.

John: Maybe you should have believed me when I said she black-mailed me.

Blake: SHE WAS SIX!

John: Clearly, she hasn't changed! But I'll forgive you for both. Although why say you wanted to try out the game when you were going to the party instead?

Blake: "Catherine invited me on the bus, so until then I was planning on trying the game out."

John: Gotcha, but why did no one else respond? I also messaged the rest of them individually. What's up with them?

Blake: I don't know. I just got my phone back and don't have anything from them either. I'll ping them and let you know if either responds.

Blake gave hourly updates, even though it was always to say he hadn't gotten any messages from the others yet.

The first half of the school day went by like any other first day back from a break: nothing was taught, and nothing was learned.

When the first lunch bell rang, the doors barely stayed on their frames as students rushed through. After the initial rush to get the good tables, John meandered around until he found his way to one of the largest trees and slumped down next to it.

He'd still had no word from either Daniel or Justin, and he was starting to get concerned all over again. Blake returning had been a nice respite, but two-thirds of your friends dropping off the face of the earth would make anyone concerned.

John sat at the base of the tree and stared at the patch of grassless dirt in front of him. He let his mind wander. He briefly flashed through some happy memories, but his brain quickly turned dark as worry took over again.

He thought of all the malicious reasons his other two friends would disappear. This continued until a voice pulled him out of his own head: his best friend, Blake. John initially recoiled slightly as he came back to reality because Blake had featured prominently in those nightmares. Instead of yelling, Blake just sat down next to him.

"Why are you just sitting here all by yourself? Don't you want to eat lunch with us?" Blake asked.

"Nah, I just want to be alone for a bit. I'll probably start reading in a minute," John responded idly.

"How are you going to read if you don't have a book with you? You left your bag back at your locker. You know, if something is wrong, you can tell me. We've been friends for more than a decade." Blake placed his hand reassuringly on John's shoulder.

After a moment of silence, John turned. "But why? Why have you dealt with me for so long? We couldn't be more different from each other. You thrive on parties and being around people; just the idea of it makes my skin crawl. You have a huge social net, while I have four people. Why hang around me if you know I won't enjoy anything you do? Why—"

"Nope," Blake said, cutting him off.

"Nope? What do you mean, nope?"

"I mean nope. It doesn't matter if you don't like everything I do; we are friends, and that ain't changing just because you would rather spend a night playing a game over going to a party. It doesn't matter that you would rather spend a night watching an entire show over going to a concert. All that matters is that we're friends and we still have—you know what? Stay right here."

Blake dashed away from the tree. Before John could fully process what he'd said, Blake brought over their two AWOL friends.

"Hey, John. Sorry about not answering you," Daniel said, rubbing the back of his neck. "I might have gotten a little angry at the party and pushed Justin's phone out of his hand and into the punch bowl. So I owed him a new one and just took the SIM card out of mine. I still don't have one now. My parents were livid, and I have to wait a month before I can get a new one."

Justin glared at Daniel. "After his tantrum, I had to get a new SIM card since punch and electronics don't go well together. So I've been trying to get all my contacts back."

"I'm sorry I bailed on you," Justin added, "but I heard that Jessica was going to be there and you know how long I've been trying to even talk to her. In order to make it up to you, we all chipped in and got you six months of game time!"

Each of his friends pulled their hands out of their pockets to show two month-long subscription cards each.

"You guys didn't need to do that," John said, choking back a few tears. "Hearing your explanations was enough."

"After we ruined your spring break, I think it was the least we could do," Blake reassured. "But . . . if you don't want them, we can always take them—"

"Nope! *Nope!* I think these will help me forgive your transgressions!"

John gathered the cards before anyone even realized he had them. As he fit the last one into his pocket, the bell rang, and the four friends stood and walked back to the school building together. John stood a bit taller and walked a bit faster, the weight on his shoulders gone and replaced by jubilation that almost made him levitate.

THREE HEADS ARE BETTER THAN ONE

Citlalin Ossio

"Your part of the loot, as promised, Risani," said a portly middle-aged man as two younger men loaded brown cloth sacks and wooden crates onto a horse-drawn wagon. "You sure this is enough?"

He raised a brow in skepticism as he looked at Risani, who stood next to him. Two buns framed her head, while the rest of her long dark-brown hair flowed in the cool evening breeze. The sunset glimmered on the crashing waves behind them.

"Don't worry, Captain. This is all I need," she answered with a bright smile. Her rustling hooded cape mirrored the sails of the *Ávinis* docked behind them. Sea air filled her lungs. "In fact, it's more than I expected. We hit the jackpot this time. I could even retire with this."

"I hope not," the captain said, alarmed.

"I'm kidding." She laughed and rested her hand on his shoulder. "I love adventuring too much to give it up."

"The cart's ready for you, Risani," said one of the younger men.

"Thanks." She climbed onto the driver's seat.

"Joo Won, go with her and keep her safe," said the captain.

"Thanks, Cap, but I can take care of myself." Risani winked.

"But it's getting dark, and I heard there are some robbers on the loose as of late. What if they try to steal from you on your way home?" His brow furrowed with worry.

"Then they'll get what's coming to them," she said with conviction and brandished a rose-gold-painted wooden boomerang from its holster. A bright round, yellow gem shimmered on the elbow.

"I'd be more worried for anyone who tries to mess with *her*. Risani can handle it, Cap," Joo Won said, trying to reassure the unconvinced captain.

"That's what worries me." Seeing that he wouldn't persuade her, he resigned. "Please at least *try* to keep out of danger."

In mock offense, Risani said, "You hurt me, Captain. I don't look for trouble. I can't help it if someone messes with me or if I see something wrong." His alarmed expression made her backtrack. "I promise I'll be safe."

His face softened. "Goodbye, Risani. Give my best to Manon."

"Aye, aye, Captain. You guys stay safe too, and don't forget to bring back some tasty treats."

Night was falling fast, but that didn't matter in the main square of the bustling port city of Wake Zost, where the night market was opening for business. Fire performers and musicians prepared acts that were best appreciated under the moon's soft light. The delicious aroma of roasting meats and fresh baked goods wafted through the air as Risani made her way past the town center to a church a few streets north.

Risani parked close to the back gates, where a resting ealin—a lion beast with feathered wings along its front legs—lifted her head at the creaking sound of the metal gates opening.

"Hey, Lalia!" Risani whispered excitedly. Her fingers barely grazed each other as she wrapped her arms around the creature's large neck. Risani rubbed her face against Lalia's soft and silky fur, which smelled like grass from her staying outside.

Lalia flicked her tail happily and purred softly as Risani rubbed her head, which was white, unlike the rest of her dark brown fur and feathers. Her dark brown paws were as big as Risani's face.

"Have you been a good guard monster and protected everyone?"

Lalia let out a deep trill as if to reassure her.

Risani removed white and brown fur from her clothes as she went to knock on the door.

She was greeted by an elderly nun, whose deeply set wrinkles were accentuated on her round, kind face when she smiled. "Risani, what a wonderful surprise."

Risani smiled cheerfully. "Good evening, Mother Superior!"

"Come in, dear. What are you doing here so late?"

"Wait, Mother Superior. First, I need help unloading some of the stuff in that wagon." She pointed behind her with her thumb. "Will you ask the kids to help me, please?"

As the oldest of the orphans strained to unload what Risani asked them to from the wagon and brought it inside, she recounted her latest adventure to the younger children, who were enthralled by her stories.

One boy, around twelve years old, was dragging a brown cloth bag behind him. He stopped to take a breath and peeked inside the bag, gasping happily when he saw the bright and shining yellow color.

"Gold!" he exclaimed.

The elderly nun gave him a stern look. "Memo! Close that bag and put it inside quickly."

Once they had finished unloading their share, Mother Superior and the children saw Risani to the gate.

One of the younger children pointed a small wet finger at the crates still in the cart. "What's in there?"

"My part of the treasure." Risani winked.

The elderly nun asked worriedly, "Are you sure you can spare so much?"

"I'm sorry to disillusion you, Mother Superior, but I'm not that selfless. I kept the best of the treasure for myself," she said with a playful laugh.

The elderly nun chuckled warmly. "You're a good girl, Risani. Thank you, as always." She hugged her, then gave Risani her blessing. "Be careful on your way home."

"Thank you. I will." Risani climbed back onto the cart and waved goodbye.

Risani lived near the Balsoro River, which passed through the city. She lived with her younger sister, Manon, who was waiting for her on the small porch of their house. Manon looked up from a thick leather-bound book, waved as Risani approached, and hurried down the steps to meet her.

Risani jumped down from her seat and hugged her sister tightly.

"Welcome home, Sis," said Manon.

"It's good to be back. Wait till you see what I got." She wore a bright smile as she hurried to the back of the cart to unload. As she unlatched the back door of the wagon, a black shuriken flew past and wedged itself in one of the wooden crates. "Whoa!" She jumped back and turned. "What?"

Three masked robbers stood a few yards away from the sisters. The masked woman on the left held another shuriken. The sharp, curved metal edges glistened menacingly between her fingers.

Manon gasped and stood behind her older sister.

The masked bandit in the middle, presumably the leader, spoke. "Listen, girls. We're tired, so let's make this quick. Back away from the cart and don't try anything stupid, and we won't hurt you."

Risani scoffed. "Oh, please." She glanced quickly at her sister. "Go inside."

"Ris." Manon hesitated.

"Go."

Manon moved back up the porch steps and went inside the house, watching the scene unfold from the window.

Risani unholstered her boomerang and tapped it against her shoulder. "Leave us alone while I'm asking nicely."

The thieves laughed. The leader raised his eyebrow. "Didn't you learn simple math? It's three against one. Lucky for you, I'm feeling generous. I'll give you one more chance. Get out of our way."

Risani let out a single astonished laugh. *I tried, Captain.* "Unlucky for you, I don't give second chances."

She threw the boomerang in a quick, graceful motion, and it

whipped through the air, hitting all three robbers in the face. They groaned in pain and grabbed their wounded heads as the boomerang returned to Risani's hand. She threw it again, hitting the one farthest to the right in the stomach. He yelled as he fell to his knees, clutching his abdomen and beating the hard ground in agony.

The masked woman had composed herself and was ready to throw a shuriken, but Risani was faster and threw her boomerang straight at the thief's hand. The woman dropped her own weapon and gripped her hand, crying from the pain. The boomerang bounced back into Risani's grasp as she ran and dove with an outstretched leg to knock the final bandit down. He got up quickly and threw his fist at Risani, but she dodged easily and punched him in the stomach before finishing him with a round-house kick.

She stepped back and smirked. "You guys up for round two?"

The robbers groaned as they stumbled to their feet and retreated back toward town, but the leader of the group stopped once to look back and glower at Risani. She waved her boomerang, wearing a bright but menacing smile, and he continued running after his comrades.

Risani yawned and stretched her arms up to the sky, then walked back to the cart.

Manon ran out and met her sister. "Are you hurt?"

"Not a scratch," answered Risani with a smug grin. She jumped into the cart and passed the crates down to her younger sister.

"Why didn't you just give them the cart?" Manon asked.

"This is my hard-earned treasure. I'm not giving it up to cowards like them."

"Is it really worth putting yourself in danger?"

"First, I wasn't in danger. Those three were punks. Second, yes. Yes, it is." Risani handed Manon the two remaining brown sacks. "This one's for Mami and Papi, and this one's for Clara and her family. The rest is for us," she finished, her eyes twinkling.

"All of it?" Manon asked in amazement.

"Believe me, this isn't going to last more than a month."

Manon nodded knowingly, then a thought hit her. "What if they come back?"

"They'll need at least ten years to catch up to my level, and by then, this'll all be gone." Risani laughed.

"What if they come back while you're gone?"

Risani held a crate in midair. "Uh, good point." She dropped the box, kicking up dirt, and spun her boomerang in her hand while she thought. Her fingers traced faint grooves in the wooden wings and the cool yellow gem in the elbow of her trusted weapon. She snapped her fingers when she got an idea. "We're going to get a guard monster."

"A guard monster?"

"Yup. I'll go to the shelter and adopt one. Then I'll train it to guard my treasure."

"You mean me?" Manon batted her eyelashes innocently.

"Sure, you too."

Manon gave her older sister an unamused side-eye. "But we've never taken care of a living creature before. What if we kill it?"

"Shouldn't you be more concerned about a monster attacking and killing us?"

"No, I'm definitely more worried about the poor creature's fate."

"Regardless." Risani waved her hand dismissively. "I'll go tomorrow morning. Those punks won't be stupid enough to try something in broad daylight."

The next day, after returning the horse-drawn cart, Risani made her way to the local shelter. The place smelled strongly of hay, grass, and dirt. A musty scent lingered in the air. She was welcomed by a woman with wavy pink and baby-blue hair tied in a ponytail.

"Welcome to Wake Zost's creature rescue shelter. How can I help you today?"

"Hello. I'm here to adopt a monster."

"Okay. What kind of creature are you looking for?"

"One that will be a good guard and protect my home."

"Would you prefer a younger or older monster?"

Risani thought for a moment and figured it'd be better to adopt a younger creature that would live longer.

The shelter employee took Risani to the young monster kennels, which housed creatures of all shapes and sizes. Most were smaller versions of those in the wild, at least the ones that could be domesticated and weren't unnecessarily violent. There was a litter of ealin cubs in one cage, huddled together as they slept. A torpi trudged around its enclosure next to them. Its spiked rock shell weighed heavily on it at that young age. Tanks covered one wall and were home to some baby water monsters, like the calmarcin, which swam around with its five tentacles.

"Some of these creatures were found injured or abandoned and brought here," explained the pink-and-blue-haired employee. "While others were dropped off because their owners could no longer care for them."

She took a baby lazorn out of its cage. The lizard-like creature's back legs and tail dangled as she held it. "This little guy was injured when we got him. See the tear?" She pointed to an injury on his front leg. "It's healing nicely, and he'll be a great companion. Lazorns are strong fighters, so he'd make an excellent guard too."

Risani looked around, and a sleeping occorii caught her attention. The three-headed puppy beast was a rare monster. It had dark fur and pointed ears and looked like a full-grown dog with two extra heads. "What about the occorii?"

"I wouldn't recommend them."

"Why not?"

"They're a handful. We haven't been able to properly train them ourselves."

"No way. They're super cute," Risani gushed.

"They are cute . . ." The employee trailed off.

"Besides, three heads are better than one, right? They'll have a wider vantage. I'll take them."

Apprehensively, the employee asked, "Have you taken care of a living creature before?"

"No. This'll be my first."

"Uh, then maybe this lazorn would be better, or perhaps even one of our older monsters that are fully trained—"

"No, I want the occorii puppy."

"But it'll be hard to train them," insisted the shelter employee.

"Miss, I've traveled across this land and others, battling all sorts of people and creatures." Confidence bordering on conceit dripped from Risani's words. "I'm well-equipped and capable of wrangling these three into shape."

The shelter employee decided to give Risani the benefit of the doubt. "Let's fill out the paperwork."

In the shelter lobby, Risani finished signing the adoption papers and handed the employee a small sack of money. She leaned against the counter as she waited for her new monster.

"In case things don't work out as you expect," started the pink-and-blue-haired employee, "you're encouraged to bring the creature back here instead of dumping it somewhere. Then we can try to find a monster better suited for you."

Risani opened her mouth to answer when a loud clatter stopped her.

"There they are," muttered the employee before the back door to the kennels flew open and the three-headed puppy emerged. Their tail wagged vigorously as they tried to run toward Risani, dragging a helpless shelter employee behind them. He held three leashes, each tied to one of the three heads.

Risani's eyes widened, and her palms began to sweat.

The pink-and-blue-haired employee stifled a laugh under her breath.

Risani cleared her throat and calmed herself.

The creature skidded to a stop at her feet, then jumped up in excitement. All three heads panted happily, their tongues sticking out.

The employee handed the leashes to Risani and ran back to the kennels before she could react.

Risani looked at the pink-and-blue-haired employee, who gave her a teasing smile. "Good luck."

Before she could respond, the occorii dragged Risani toward the exit, and soon she was out the door.

Outside, Risani tried her best to pull the monster where she wanted to go, but to no avail. Frustrated, she stopped walking, put her fingers in her mouth, and whistled.

The occarii turned and ran toward her, bouncing with young energy.

"Sit. Sit!" demanded Risani, pushing their bottom down.

They sat, but their fluffy tail continued to wag excitedly as they looked up at their owner through dark brown eyes. The head in the middle had one eye that was a lighter shade of brown than the rest.

"All right, you three, listen up," she started in a stern voice. "I'm in charge, so you're going to obey me and—no, look at me," she said as their attention shifted toward a sound across the street. They faced her again, and Risani continued. "You're going to listen to me, and you're not going to give me any trouble. Understand?"

All three puppy heads panted happily.

"Good." She smiled. "Let's go." She tugged their leashes in the opposite direction and started home.

The usually twenty-minute walk back took nearly an hour as the baby monster dragged Risani up and down the streets to investigate every new thing they heard or smelled.

Manon, who was watching from the window, laughed when she saw her usually confident sister struggling to control the three-headed puppy as Risani made her way to the house. Manon opened the door for them, squealing, "Oh my goodness! They're so cute."

The creature bounced enthusiastically, barking with joy.

Risani dropped the leashes and collapsed against the closed door. "Their cuteness wears off," she said in between pants.

The occorii pounced on Risani and gifted her with wet kisses.

"Ah! Get off, get off!" She scrambled to her feet. "Ugh, nasty!" she complained, wiping her face with her cape.

Manon laughed and rubbed the three-headed puppy's back. "Good job!"

The puppies settled down enough to explore their new home, trotting around the house and sniffing everything. The sisters followed closely behind.

"What's their name?" asked Manon.

"They don't have one yet. Any suggestions?"

Manon thought for a moment. "Do you want to give each head a separate name?"

"Mm, no. It'll be too confusing. Besides, it's not like we can call on just one. How about a three-syllable word for their name? Like bibimbap, tortilla, or spaghetti."

"Of course your brain goes immediately to food. Do you think with your stomach?"

Risani laughed, unashamed.

"Hmm, let's see. Three-syllables . . ."

"There's also banana and upanva. Mmm. That last one tastes really good." Risani licked her lips.

"Great, now all I can think of is food." Manon paused. "Ah! Keeping with that theme, how about Camote? You love them, especially when Mami makes them into candy. You could finish a whole box by yourself. You have, actually."

"Camote? Camote," repeated Risani, feeling out the name. "Camote."

The puppies cocked their heads.

Risani emphasized every syllable, "Ca-Mo-Te."

The puppies barked and wagged their tail.

"Do you guys like that name?"

The occorii spun in a circle and barked again.

Risani took that as a yes. "Camote it is, then."

"Welcome to the family, Camote," said Manon, rubbing their new pet's back.

The creature's body trembled with excitement.

Risani looked at the clock. "Aren't you going to school?" she asked Manon.

"I can stay and help you today."

"Don't worry about me. I survived the hardest part, getting them here. I can manage."

"Are you sure?"

"Yes, go." Risani insisted.

"Mm, okay," said Manon, unconvinced.

Risani saw her sister to the door, and Camote followed closely behind. She gave Manon a goodbye kiss on her cheek. "Be careful. Love you."

"Love you too, Sis," responded Manon. "See you later." Then she bent down and rubbed Camote's three heads. In a gushing voice, she said, "Goodbye, Camote. See you later."

The puppies panted happily and licked Manon's arms. She giggled at their ticklish touch.

Risani closed the door and turned to Camote. "Okay, buddies," she said, hands on her hips. "Time for lesson one."

She took Camote to the door of her treasure room. "Behind this door is where I keep my most precious loot from my latest adventure. I'm going to train you to guard what's inside it from people who want to steal it when I'm not here."

The occorii heads sniffed at the crack at the bottom of the door, and they wagged their tail. They pawed at the door, whining to get inside.

"Not yet." Risani pulled on their leashes. "Come on." She took Camote to the back door. "Wait here while I change into a thief."

Risani came back with her face masked face and wearing darker clothes. She wore padded training clothes to protect her when it was time to teach Camote to attack. She stopped in her tracks when she realized the puppy was nowhere in sight. "Camote?"

She moved around the house, calling out their name. "Camote, where are you?" She entered the living room and gasped. The couch cushions were shredded and torn, and the three puppy heads fought over a pillow.

She pulled down her mask. "Hey! Drop it!" She grabbed the pillow, but the occorii struggled against her grip until the pillow ripped and stuffing filled the air. She stared at the fabric in her hand, stunned, then shot Camote an angry look. "You three are in so much trouble."

Camote whined and lowered their heads. Their tail hung low.

Risani let out a heavy sigh as she assessed the damage. The couch cushions weren't the sole casualty; the coffee table's wooden legs were covered in bite marks. Miraculously, a vase of flowers teetered on the edge of the table but hadn't fallen.

"I'll clean this up later. First, let's go outside before you three start in on the dining table."

She grabbed Camote's three leashes. Going into the kitchen, she grabbed a half loaf of bread that sat on the counter and stuffed it in her satchel.

All three puppies lifted their snouts and sniffed the air in anticipation. Their tail whipped through the air.

"Let's go," said Risani. She headed out to the backyard, and Camote followed hurriedly and without complaint.

She left Camote at one end of the backyard, expecting the occorii to stay put, but when she looked back, Camote was standing next to her. "No, you have to stay over there." She pointed to the other side of the lawn. "Go back."

But Camote remained at her side, their tongues lolling. Drool hung from the sides of their mouths.

Risani sighed heavily. "Okay, let's start with that." She took a piece of bread from her bag and held it in her palm. "Sit." Risani pushed her hand toward Camote's back.

The puppy heads followed the smell of the food with their snouts and, in doing so, sat on their bottom.

"Good job!" Risani let go of the bread, and Mo, the puppy in the middle, was the lucky one to catch the treat. Ca and Te, the two on the ends, protested with low, frustrated growls, baring their teeth.

"Oh! Sorry, sorry. That's my bad," said Risani, quickly ripping two more pieces of bread. She fed the two puppies on the ends, and they returned to their happy selves. Risani looked at the small loaf of bread and realized she'd underestimated how much she would need.

Camote learned to sit on command quickly, but it took the remainder of the bread for them to learn to stay.

"There's no more," said Risani, turning her hands to show Camote. "I'll go get something else. Stay," she commanded before leaving. She darted inside and grabbed the first food she saw, a bunch of bananas. She ran outside, and to her surprise and relief, Camote was in the same place she had left them. Mo was grooming Ca's neck, while Te was sniffing a flower by their foot.

Risani smiled proudly. She peeled a banana and split it in three parts as she walked toward them. "I'll give you guys extra since you did a good job."

She gave each a piece of the fruit, and they wolfed it down after one or two bites. They looked at her expectantly.

Risani laughed, dumbfounded. "You guys should have chewed it more. All right, next lesson. I'm going to act like a robber, so you have to attack me." She found two fallen branches and tapped them together as she moved toward Camote to agitate them. She growled and yelled as she moved closer.

Camote bowed in a playful manner and ran toward her, their mouths wide open. Risani dropped the branches and braced herself for them to bite her. But instead of biting her arm, they jumped up and licked her face.

"No! No! Stop, Camote." Risani pushed them off her. "I'm a thief right now. You have to attack me." She walked a few steps but turned when she heard Camote following her. "Stay."

They stayed in place, their tail wagging.

Risani picked up the branches. "Let's try this again." She faced Camote and hit the branches together harder and screamed louder as she enticed them to chase and attack her.

They ran toward her. When they were about to reach her, Risani turned and ran away from them, making Camote chase after her. She continued to hit the sticks together and yell while Camote barked eagerly. Risani answered their barks with joyful laughter. She turned to run backward so she could agitate Camote further, but she tripped and fell on her back. Camote stood over her and licked her face.

"Ah! No!" Risani rushed to her feet and wiped the warm saliva off with her sleeves. Camote grabbed the sticks and tugged at them, breaking one.

Risani sighed. "Maybe I should've accepted Manon's help. This might be harder than I thought."

After a few hours of minimal improvement, Risani and Camote

were wiped out from the running and took a break. Risani sat on the grass, running her hands along Camote's soft fur. The puppies' tongues lolled from their mouths, and their body shook from their exhausted panting.

Risani went inside and filled three wooden bowls with water. She placed one in front of each of Camote's heads. "Drink up."

Camote splashed water onto the ground as they lapped the cool refreshment. Ca finished its portion and licked its mouth, while Mo and Te let excess water drip from theirs.

Risani stretched and, looking up at the sky, realized Manon would be home soon and she still hadn't cleaned up Camote's living room redecoration. "I better clean it up before Manon gets home and has a panic attack."

Camote stood up to follow her.

"Oh, no. You three stay out here. At least if you destroy the flower beds, they're easier to fix." With horror, she realized what she had said and looked at each pair of brown eyes in turn. "That's not an invitation."

Risani sighed heavily when she entered the living room. "I hate cleaning." She gathered the stuffing that seemed to have exploded onto everything in sight. Then Risani took the couch cushions and flipped them upside down. She shrugged. "She'll never know." As for the destroyed pillow, Risani hoped Manon wouldn't notice it was missing. She took a blanket from her dresser and draped it over the ruined coffee table. The sheet barely covered the legs. "It's fine. It's fine," she said, trying to convince herself.

Risani finished tidying up the living room just as Manon opened the front door. She tossed the brown sack full of stuffing behind the couch.

"Camote!" Manon called expectantly from the foyer. "Camote."

"Did you forget about me?" asked Risani as she emerged from the living room. "Your sister?"

"I've seen you almost every day for twenty years. The excitement of seeing you only comes after you've been gone a long time. So where's Camote? Camote!" She walked around, looking for them.

"Replaced by a dog," Risani said, dumbfounded, and shook her head. "They're outside."

Manon gasped. "Why did you leave them outside? Poor guys," she said worriedly as she made her way to the back door. "It's so muggy. They'd be more comfortable in here."

Risani pursed her lips. She clenched her fists and took a deep breath to control herself before following Manon outside.

"Camote!" Manon called as she exited into the backyard.

They were nowhere in sight.

Risani's stomach churned anxiously. "Oh, no." She walked around her sister and searched frantically, praying for that they hadn't gotten into trouble again. "Camote! Camote!" she called as she searched. She rounded the corner of the house and found the occorii lying on the ground behind a bush. "Camote, what are you—" She gasped. "Camote, what did you do?"

The puppies' legs and stomach were covered in mud. Their wet fur stuck out in small clumps, and they splashed muddy water as they pawed frantically at a puddle. Their three snouts were drenched brown from pulling and tugging at roots inside the murky water.

"What? What happened?" Manon asked as she rushed to the side of the house. She also gasped and covered her mouth upon seeing Camote's latest mischievous act. She noticed Risani's sunken shoulders shaking. "Ris, it's okay. We can clean them up."

Risani tilted her head back and laughed hysterically. She held her stomach as tears rolled down her cheeks, and she spoke in between laughs. "I can't do this anymore. These three are too much, even for me." She paused to suck in air. "I should have listened to the shelter employee and gotten the lazorn." She wiped tears from her eyes.

"Ris?"

Camote skipped over to them and shook their body, spraying Risani and Manon with mud.

"Ahh!" Risani yelled. Camote inched toward her, but she pulled away. "No. Bad Camote!"

The occorii whimpered, and their ears and tail lowered.

"I really can't do this, Manon. It's impossible to train them. I'm taking them back to the shelter, where they can be someone else's problem. I'll get another monster."

"Wait, wait. You can't give up. That's not your style. Besides, you love a challenge."

"Ha! They're not just a challenge. They're a headache, a pain in the neck, and a thorn in my side, all rolled into one!"

"Have you eaten?"

"No."

"Ah, okay," Manon said knowingly. "Go eat something and take a break while I wash them up."

"They will destroy you."

"Stop exaggerating and go eat, please."

Risani listened to her sister and grabbed a bite to eat. She watched Manon give Camote a bath. Every time she dumped a bucket of water over them, they shook their body, splashing Manon with soapy water.

Risani went back out with towels as Manon poured a final bucket of water over Camote. She stood at a safe distance as, on cue, Camote shook their body. Manon was completely drenched. Risani handed her a towel.

"Thanks." Manon started drying Camote.

"That was for you. Here." Risani exchanged the dry towel for the damp one. She finished drying Camote, who panted happily. Their fur shone and smelled of lavender and vanilla.

"Feeling rational again?" Manon asked as she dried her short brown hair.

"Yeah," Risani admitted grudgingly.

Manon laughed. "You always get a little dramatic when you're hungry."

Risani dried Camote's back. "Sorry for going crazy earlier. But if you three want to stay, you need to work with me."

Te gave a surprise lick to her face.

Risani pursed her lips and wiped the spit off with her shoulder. She was getting used to their slimy kisses.

"I can stay home tomorrow and help you train them," offered Manon.

Risani sighed resignedly. "That's probably best."

Manon wrapped her arm around Risani's slumped shoulders. "You can't do everything by yourself, Sis."

"I would've disagreed with you before today."

The sisters watched as Ca pulled its siblings to a fallen oak branch. Ca picked up one end while Te grabbed the other. They engaged up in a tug-of-war, while Mo just watched them.

"I was tricked," said Risani. "They looked like angels when they were asleep."

Camote got bored of the stick and dropped it. They searched the backyard for a new amusement. They sniffed the soil near a patch of flowers. Their ears perked up, and they pushed their faces deeper into the flower bed and dug desperately.

"Hey!" yelled Risani, scrambling to her feet. She pulled on their collars. "I told you guys not to do that!"

They ignored her and continued to scratch at the dirt.

Manon covered her face in resignation but peeked through her fingers.

"Camote!" said Risani in a complaining tone.

Then a squirrel squeaked, catching the occorii's attention, and they chased after the rodent, pulling Risani with them.

"Whoa!" she yelled as she let go of their collars and fell on her face.

Manon rushed to her side. "Ris!"

Risani sat up and laughed.

Camote lost the squirrel, so they ran back to the girls.

Risani saw their tongues and yelled playfully as she stood and ran away from them. Camote chased after her, and they played until the sun lowered beneath the horizon.

"Why can't they sleep inside?" Manon asked as Risani tied Camote's leashes to an oak tree.

"Not until they're fully trained," Risani answered.

Manon rubbed her arms to warm herself. "But it gets cold at night."

Camote whined as they struggled against their restraints.

"I brought a blanket; they'll be fine. Now stop feeling guilty. They can sense it." Risani looked at Camote. "This is only temporary. Let this be motivation for you guys to learn fast." She patted each head and wrapped them with the blanket.

The puppies whimpered as the sisters went inside and left them alone.

As the girls were getting ready for bed, Camote continued to cry and howl.

Manon peeked out from behind the curtains and bit her lip.

"Just ignore them," said Risani. "They'll get tired eventually and fall asleep."

But two hours later, Camote was still going strong, barking and howling without end.

"Ris, I can't listen to this anymore. Please just bring them inside."

"If I showed you the mess they made in the living room, you'd think differently. They'll stop soon enough. They can't possibly go the whole night." At least, she hoped so.

Loud banging on the front door made the girls jump.

Worried, Manon asked, "Who's that?"

"Stay here. I'll go check."

Risani peeked through the small window in the front door, and her heart sank to her stomach. She saw the twisted, angry face of their elderly Camafol neighbor. His small black eyes squinted in annoyance, and his scales reddened.

Risani swallowed down the lump in her throat and opened the door. "Good evening, Mr. Luc Aro." She smiled sheepishly.

"How good of an evening could it be with that creature's incessant barking?"

"I'm sorry for the noise."

He pointed his wooden cane at Risani. "You better quiet that beast, Risani, or I'll do it for you."

"Y-yes, Mr. Luc Aro."

He harrumphed and waddled back down the steps. His twisty tail trailed behind him.

Risani ran outside, and Camote jumped excitedly.

"You three need to be quiet and go to sleep."

They yipped happily.

"Shh!"

Camote stopped and panted.

Risani breathed a sigh of relief.

Then all three heads sniffed the air and looked behind Risani. To her horror, they started barking again. They stood in a rigid posture, and the fur along their back stood up.

"Camote, be quiet! If you three don't listen to me, I'm really going to take you back—" She stopped when they bared their teeth and growled, finally realizing something was wrong. She turned around and saw a group of eight masked people around her.

"Hello again," said the one in the middle, waving his hand.

Risani recognized his voice.

"We're back for round two, and this time, we brought our siblings to help." He chuckled smugly.

Risani instinctively grabbed for her boomerang, but with mounting horror, she realized she had left it in the house. She hid her disappointment. "I told you I don't give second warnings."

"I remember, so I won't waste time. Get her!"

Half the thieves charged at Risani.

Camote pulled desperately against their leashes, snarling and barking.

Risani waited for the bandits to get closer, then did a handstand and spun her legs through the air, knocking the thieves down. She stood and kicked another robber who ran toward her. Then one grabbed her from behind. She pushed against him to jump and kick another masked person, then stepped hard on the first thief's foot, elbowing him in the stomach. He let go and fell to the ground, groaning.

Risani's victory was short-lived. A bandit hit her from behind, and Risani's cheek hit the hard ground as she fell. Her head throbbed. She coughed and tasted iron. A few drops of blood rolled down her jaw. Hot pain raced up her arms as two masked men yanked her up and held her.

Camote jumped and tugged even harder to escape. Their leather leashes began to pull and crack.

The leader of the gang laughed as Risani struggled against the thieves' tight hold. "Ready to hand over my treasure?"

"You're all cowards."

"We saw you give part of the treasure to the church. We're just asking for the same generosity," he said in mock innocence. He noticed Camote. "Looks like you got yourself a monster. Much good it does, tied up like that." He laughed. "Actually, we couldn't take the bigger share of the treasure you gave to the church because of the ealin guarding them, so we settled for what you had left. But I admit, I underestimated you." He unsheathed a small blade and walked toward Risani. "But now you're outnumbered and outmatched."

Risani clenched her fist as he pressed the cool metal to her neck.

"So stop wasting my time and give me my treasure."

Camote jumped and pulled fiercely against their leashes, and finally the leather snapped and broke. They ran straight at the two thieves who held Risani. They opened their jaws and bit down hard, sinking their teeth into the two robbers' legs.

The masked bandits screamed loud, high-pitched shrieks of pain. They fell to the ground, clutching their legs and crying as blood ran down their dark pants and pooled under them.

"Wha—" The leader backed up, as did others, while some were frozen in place.

Camote moved in front of Risani, their ears pinned back. They bared their teeth and growled threateningly.

"Ris!"

Risani turned to Manon, who called from the back door, waving her boomerang. Manon threw it, and Risani caught it. The familiar feel of the wooden grains gave Risani a surge of confidence, and she threw it at the frozen thieves.

They groaned and clutched their bodies where the boomerang hit them. Two immediately ran away.

One tried to attack Camote but cowered back, screaming, when the occorii lunged at her. She ran away in such a rush that she tripped and fell. Other robbers dragged their two injured comrades, the ones who had been bitten by Camote. They cried and groaned loudly, leaving trails of blood as they were carried away.

"Come back!" yelled the leader.

Camote growled at him and got low, ready to pounce.

The leader waved his blade with a shaky hand.

Risani smirked and threw her boomerang, disarming him.

"Ah!" He clutched his hand. He ran away, but Camote chased after him. In his hurry, the leader tripped on a rock and fell face-first into the grass. He turned onto his back and yelled as Camote jumped on him, mouths open.

"Camote, stay!"

Camote bared their teeth and growled lowly at the shaking thief under their paws. Saliva dripped from their mouths, hitting the leader's face and mask.

Risani moved toward them and called for the puppies. "Camote, come here."

The puppies gave a few final loud and aggressive barks before getting off the thief, who scrambled to his feet and ran away without looking back. Camote watched until he was out of sight before relaxing and running to Risani.

She bent down and hugged them. "Good job, you guys!" She released them and rubbed their necks.

The puppies yipped happily.

Manon rushed to their side and hugged her sister. "Are you okay?"

"For the most part." She rubbed her head gingerly and wiped blood from her lips. "Thanks to Camote."

Manon hugged the occorii. "Thank you, Camote. You did great."

Camote sat down and scratched Ca's neck with their hind leg, then they shook their body. They barked again, and their tongues lolled as they panted in excitement.

"You three are naturals," said Risani. "With more training, you'll be the best guard monsters in town, and no one will dare mess with us."

"So we're definitely keeping them?"

"Of course!"

Manon asked hopefully, "And they can sleep inside?"

"Uh . . ." Risani looked into Camote's three pairs of brown eyes. "Yeah." She rubbed their necks and scratched behind their ears. "They deserve it. Besides, we'll never get any sleep otherwise." She laughed. "We can buy new furniture later."

The girls took Camote inside, and as they passed Risani's treasure room, Manon laughed. "Imagine the looks on the robbers' faces had they seen the *grand* treasure you're keeping," she teased.

"Admit it, those exotic foods are delicious," said Risani.

"The purple one is good, but I didn't really like the bread. It had too much cheese. And I don't like the watermelon dessert."

"Ah, my poor uncultured sister. You should look up from your books more often."

Camote again pawed at the door to Risani's treasure room. They wagged their tail.

Risani said, "I don't trust you in there yet, but I'll give you guys some delicious treats tomorrow."

The sisters laughed as they walked to their room, Camote following, tail wagging.

Risani climbed into bed and pulled the covers over her. Then Camote jumped up and settled by her feet. "Hey! Get off." She tried to push Camote down, but they wouldn't budge.

Manon laughed.

"You guys are hogging the bed," Risani complained as she gave up and laid on her pillow.

"Good night, Sis. Good night, Camote," said Manon.

"Good night," Risani responded, yawning.

The puppies stood and turned in a circle to get more comfortable. They yawned in turns, then laid their heads on Risani's legs.

She smiled and gave each one a last pat on their heads. Through a crack in the curtains, the moon shone on the sleeping puppies' faces.

They are pretty cute.

THE AUTHORS

Stephanie Adams has too many passions and hobbies for her own good. Although she has a doctorate in pharmacy, she's currently taking a break to stay at home and hang out with her awesome 4 year old. She enjoys painting, gardening, photography, baking, crafts, and writing when she can grab a random minute to herself. Continually inspired by her son, she's presently working on writing children's books. Stephanie lives in North Carolina with her husband, son, and a stray cat that likes to show up randomly and sunbathe on their porch.

Stephen Adams is a software developer and podcaster. He spends the vast majority of his time flipping bits for his day job and yelling into a microphone for the 2Dorks family of podcasts and twitch streams. He primarily reads and writes fantasy and sci-fi, because where else can you find giant space worms or an angry dragon with a particularly painful hang nail? When not writing or making content on the internet, Stephen is hanging out with his unbelievably supportive family at their home in North Carolina. To find out more about Stephen, visit https://about.me/stevehnh.

Rebekah Aman is the author of the young adult, fantasy series Keepers of the Essence, which currently has four books available (www.keepersoftheessence.com). In addition to writing, she works as an accountant in Tallahassee, Florida. She also enjoys singing and has performed in several musicals, some of which include The Sound of Music, Marvelous Wonderettes, and Beehive. She is grateful to have been given the opportunity to join this monster clean-up project that challenged her to branch out into a chilling new genre.

Kelly Lynn Colby is a writer of all things fantasy. Whenever she tries to create a mundane story, a dragon pops in to take over. She eventually stopped fighting and caved to the magic. The dragons must have known something she didn't, because her debut novel, *Tarbin's True Heir*, won a bronze medal in the IPPYs for fantasy. You can find her short stories in *Eclectically Heroic*, *Eclectically Magical*, *Cursed Collectibles*, and *Winter Whimsy*. If you want to read more by Kelly, check out her website at https://kellylynncolby.com or connect on Twitter @kcolbywrites.

Ben Collins wasn't planning on writing a submission, but inspiration struck in class when he was studying for a test. After writing just the first paragraph, he fell in love with it. Ben spent two and sometimes three class periods a day working on it. The ability to write something he hasn't been able to in about six years, fiction, was a refreshing breath of air for him. The prompt of a monster and its mess got him to try and find some way to give it unique spin and turn it on its head. If you want to know when he will have another story, so does he.

While not procrastinating to the full extent of her being, **A.F. Hartsell** can be found co-hosting her podcast Horseshoes and Hand Grenades, hitting the keys on next writing adventure, engaging in spirited bouts of Dungeons and Dragons, or fast asleep. If you would like to hear more from Ashley, join her on Twitter @Phatekills.

A scientist by training, **Jacob Hartsell** spends most of his days watching fishing-related videos, brewing gallons of beer, and producing Horseshoes and Hand Grenades podcast. He enjoys golfing, but sacrifices time on the green for time spent working on the money pit he fondly calls home. Jacob dreams of one day being finished with renovations so that he may dedicate more time to his Wagyu beef fetish.

David Neilsen is the author of two Middle Grade horror/comic/fantasies published by Crown Books for Young Readers: *Dr. Fell and the Playground of Doom* (2016) and *Beyond the Doors* (2017). A classically trained actor, David works as a professional storyteller based in Sleepy Hollow, NY and spends much of October spooking the bejeebers out of people or performing one of his one-man shows inspired by the works of H. P. Lovecraft. He lives with his wife, son, daughter, and two very domineering cats.

Citlalin Ossio is a hungry panda, who graduated from the University of Houston with a degree in Media Production in 2016. She was a 2017 Women in Horror Film Festival finalist for her screenplay adaptation of Meg Hafdahl's short story Guts. She is a Mexican-American whose hours of playing video games, especially Legend of Zelda games, and watching anime and Korean dramas (which she justifies as "storytelling research") fueled her desire to write fantasies and rom-coms. She lives in Houston, Texas and loves eating, being with her family, creating art in whatever medium, and plotting new ways to make the universe fall in love with pandas.

ACKNOWLEDGMENTS

I am so grateful to so many people for making this anthology possible. It's the first book for a brand-new publishing company. I can't think of a better way to start a business than to help children in need.

First, I'd like to thank the 2Dorks—Stephen, Ashley, and Jacob—for forming a supportive community of creative people. You are the best!

I have to thank our copy editor, Dorothy Tinker, for making sure we got the grammar as accurate as possible at a charity-friendly rate. If you need an editor, developmental or copy, you couldn't do better than D Tinker Editing.

Most of all, I need to thank my husband, Kevin, without whom I'd be lost. He's a partner in the new company, with jobs ranging from spreadsheets to website to keeping me from freaking out. Cursed Dragon Ship Publishing, LLC would not be a thing if not for this amazing man.

Finally, I'd like to thank all the readers who took a chance and decided to help the children.